# BETWEEN THE DARK AND THE DAYLIGHT

## *Romances*

WILLIAM DEAN HOWELLS

1st WORLD
LIBRARY
Literary Society

# Between The Dark And The Daylight

## William Dean Howells

© 1st World Library, 2007
PO Box 2211
Fairfield, IA 52556
www.1stworldlibrary.com
First Edition

LCCN: 2007920703

Softcover ISBN: 978-1-4218-4017-8
Hardcover ISBN: 978-1-4218-3917-2
eBook ISBN: 978-1-4218-4117-5

Purchase *"Between The Dark And The Daylight"*
as a traditional bound book at:
www.1stWorldLibrary.com/purchase.asp?ISBN=978-1-4218-4017-8

1st World Library is a literary, educational organization
dedicated to:

- Creating a free internet library of downloadable ebooks

- Hosting writing competitions and offering book
  publishing scholarships.

Interested in more 1st World Library books?
contact: literacy@1stworldlibrary.com
Check us out at: www.1stworldlibrary.com

# 1$^{st}$ World Library Literary Society

## Giving Back to the World

"If you want to work on the core problem, it's early school literacy."

**- James Barksdale, former CEO of Netscape**

"No skill is more crucial to the future of a child, or to a democratic and prosperous society, than literacy."

**- Los Angeles Times**

Literacy... means far more than learning how to read and write... The aim is to transmit... knowledge and promote social participation."

**- UNESCO**

"Literacy is not a luxury, it is a right and a responsibility. If our world is to meet the challenges of the twenty-first century we must harness the energy and creativity of all our citizens."

**- President Bill Clinton**

"Parents should be encouraged to read to their children, and teachers should be equipped with all available techniques for teaching literacy, so the varying needs and capacities of individual kids can be taken into account."

**- Hugh Mackay**

# CONTENTS

I

## A SLEEP AND A FORGETTING

I

Matthew Lanfear had stopped off, between Genoa and Nice, at San Remo in the interest of a friend who had come over on the steamer with him, and who wished him to test the air before settling there for the winter with an invalid wife. She was one of those neurasthenics who really carry their climate—always a bad one—with them, but she had set her mind on San Remo; and Lanfear was willing to pass a few days in the place making the observations which he felt pretty sure would be adverse.

His train was rather late, and the sunset was fading from the French sky beyond the Italian shore when he got out of his car and looked round for a porter to take his valise. His roving eye lighted on the anxious figure, which as fully as the anxious face, of a short, stout, elderly man expressed a sort of distraction, as he stood loaded down with umbrellas, bags, bundles, and wraps, and seemed unable to arrest the movements of a tall young girl, with a travelling-shawl trailing from her arm, who had the effect of escaping from him towards a bench beside the door of the waiting-room. When she reached it, in spite of his appeals, she sat down with an absent air, and looked as far withdrawn from the bustle of the platform and from the snuffling train as if on some quiet garden seat along with her own thoughts.

In his fat frenzy, which Lanfear felt to be pathetic, the old gentleman glanced at him, and then abruptly demanded: "Are you an American?"

We knew each other abroad in some mystical way, and Lanfear did not try to deny the fact.

"Oh, well, then," the stranger said, as if the fact made everything right, "will you kindly tell my daughter, on that bench by the door yonder"—he pointed with a bag, and dropped a roll of rugs from under his arm—"that I'll be with her as soon as I've looked after the trunks? Tell her not to move till I come. Heigh! Here! Take hold of these, will you?" He caught the sleeve of a *facchino* who came wandering by, and heaped him with his burdens, and then pushed ahead of the man in the direction of the baggage-room with a sort of mastery of the situation which struck Lanfear as springing from desperation rather than experience.

Lanfear stood a moment hesitating. Then a glance at the girl on the bench, drooping a little forward in freeing her face from the veil that hung from her pretty hat, together with a sense of something quaintly charming in the confidence shown him on such purely compatriotic grounds, decided him to do just what he had been asked. The girl had got her veil up by this time, and as he came near, she turned from looking at the sunset over the stretch of wall beyond the halting train, and met his dubious face with a smile.

"It *is* beautiful, isn't it?" she said. "I know I shall get well, here, if they have such sunsets every day."

There was something so convincingly normal in her expression that Lanfear dismissed a painful conjecture. "I beg your pardon," he said. "I am afraid there's some mistake. I haven't the pleasure—You must excuse me, but your father wished me to ask you to wait here for him till he had got his baggage—"

"My father?" the girl stopped him with a sort of a frowning

William Dean Howells

perplexity in the stare she gave him. "My father isn't here!"

"I beg your pardon," Lanfear said. "I must have misunderstood. A gentleman who got out of the train with you—a short, stout gentleman with gray hair—I understood him to say you were his daughter—requested me to bring this message—"

The girl shook her head. "I don't know him. It must be a mistake."

"The mistake is mine, no doubt. It may have been some one else whom he pointed out, and I have blundered. I'm very sorry if I seem to have intruded—"

"What place is this?" the girl asked, without noticing his excuses.

"San Remo," Lanfear answered. "If you didn't intend to stop here, your train will be leaving in a moment."

"I meant to get off, I suppose," she said. "I don't believe I'm going any farther." She leaned back against the bars of the bench, and put up one of her slim arms along the top.

There was something wrong. Lanfear now felt that, in spite of her perfect tranquillity and self-possession; perhaps because of it. He had no business to stay there talking with her, but he had not quite the right to leave her, though practically he had got his dismissal, and apparently she was quite capable of taking care of herself, or could have been so in a country where any woman's defencelessness was not any man's advantage. He could not go away without some effort to be of use.

"I beg your pardon," he said. "Can I help you in calling a carriage; or looking after your hand-baggage—it will be getting dark—perhaps your maid—"

"My *maid*!" The girl frowned again, with a measure of the

amazement which she showed when he mentioned her father. "*I* have no maid!"

Lanfear blurted desperately out: "You are alone? You came—you are going to stay here—alone?"

"Quite alone," she said, with a passivity in which there was no resentment, and no feeling unless it were a certain color of dignity. Almost at the same time, with a glance beside and beyond him, she called out joyfully: "Ah, there you are!" and Lanfear turned, and saw scuffling and heard puffing towards them the short, stout elderly gentleman who had sent him to her. "I knew you would come before long!"

"Well, I thought it was pretty long, myself," the gentleman said, and then he courteously referred himself to Lanfear. "I'm afraid this gentleman has found it rather long, too; but I couldn't manage it a moment sooner."

Lanfear said: "Not at all. I wish I could have been of any use to—"

"My daughter—Miss Gerald, Mr.—"

"Lanfear—Dr. Lanfear," he said, accepting the introduction; and the girl bowed.

"Oh, doctor, eh?" the father said, with a certain impression. "Going to stop here?"

"A few days," Lanfear answered, making way for the forward movement which the others began.

"Well, well! I'm very much obliged to you, very much, indeed; and I'm sure my daughter is."

The girl said, "Oh yes, indeed," rather indifferently, and then as they passed him, while he stood lifting his hat, she turned radiantly on him. "Thank you, ever so much!" she said, with the gentle voice which he had already thought charming.

The father called back: "I hope we shall meet again. We are going to the Sardegna."

Lanfear had been going to the Sardegna himself, but while he bowed he now decided upon another hotel.

The mystery, whatever it was, that the brave, little, fat father was carrying off so bluffly, had clearly the morbid quality of unhealth in it, and Lanfear could not give himself freely to a young pleasure in the girl's dark beauty of eyes and hair, her pale, irregular, piquant face, her slender figure and flowing walk. He was in the presence of something else, something that appealed to his scientific side, to that which was humane more than that which was human in him, and abashed him in the other feeling. Unless she was out of her mind there was no way of accounting for her behavior, except by some caprice which was itself scarcely short of insanity. She must have thought she knew him when he approached, and when she addressed him those first words; but when he had tried to set her right he had not changed; and why had she denied her father, and then hailed him with joy when he came back to her? She had known that she intended to stop at San Remo, but she had not known where she had stopped when she asked what place it was. She was consciously an invalid of some sort, for she spoke of getting well under sunsets like that which had now waned, but what sort of invalid was she?

## II

Lanfear's question persisted through the night, and it helped, with the coughing in the next room, to make a bad night for him. None of the hotels in San Remo receive consumptive patients, but none are without somewhere a bronchial cough. If it is in the room next yours it keeps you awake, but it is not pulmonary; you may comfort yourself in your vigils with that fact. Lanfear, however, fancied he had got a poor dinner, and in the morning he did not like his coffee. He thought he had let a foolish scruple keep him from the Grand Hotel Sardegna, and he walked down towards it along the palm-flanked promenade, in the gay morning light, with the tideless sea on the other hand lapping the rough beach beyond the lines of the railroad which borders it. On his way he met files of the beautiful Ligurian women, moving straight under the burdens balanced on their heads, or bestriding the donkeys laden with wine-casks in the roadway, or following beside the carts which the donkeys drew. Ladies of all nations, in the summer fashions of London, Berlin, St. Petersburg, Paris, and New York thronged the path. The sky was of a blue so deep, so liquid that it seemed to him he could scoop it in his hand and pour it out again like water. Seaward, he glanced at the fishing-boats lying motionless in the offing, and the coastwise steamer that runs between Nice and Genoa trailing a thin plume of smoke between him and their white sails. With the more definite purpose of making sure of the Grand Hotel Sardegna, he scanned the different villa slopes that showed their level lines of white and yellow and dull pink through the gray tropical greenery on the different levels of the hills. He was duly rewarded by the sight of the bold legend topping its cornice, and when he let his eye descend the garden to a little pavilion on the wall overlooking the road, he saw his acquaintances of the evening before making a belated breakfast. The father recognized Lanfear first and spoke to his daughter, who looked up from her coffee and down towards him where he wavered, lifting his hat, and bowed smiling to him. He had no reason to cross the roadway towards the white stairway which

William Dean Howells

climbed from it to the hotel grounds, but he did so. The father leaned out over the wall, and called down to him: "Won't you come up and join us, doctor?"

"Why, yes!" Lanfear consented, and in another moment he was shaking hands with the girl, to whom, he noticed, her father named him again. He had in his glad sense of her white morning dress and her hat of green-leafed lace, a feeling that she was somehow meeting him as a friend of indefinite date in an intimacy unconditioned by any past or future time. Her pleasure in his being there was as frank as her father's, and there was a pretty trust of him in every word and tone which forbade misinterpretation.

"I was just talking about you, doctor," the father began, "and saying what a pity you hadn't come to our hotel. It's a capital place."

"*I've* been thinking it was a pity I went to mine," Lanfear returned, "though I'm in San Remo for such a short time it's scarcely worth while to change."

"Well, perhaps if you came here, you might stay longer. I guess we're booked for the winter, Nannie?" He referred the question to his daughter, who asked Lanfear if he would not have some coffee.

"I was going to say I had had my coffee, but I'm not sure it *was* coffee," Lanfear began, and he consented, with some demur, banal enough, about the trouble.

"Well, that's right, then, and no trouble at all," Mr. Gerald broke in upon him. "Here comes a fellow looking for a chance to bring you some," and he called to a waiter wandering distractedly about with a "Heigh!" that might have been offensive from a less obviously inoffensive man. "Can you get our friend here a cup and saucer, and some of this good coffee?" he asked, as the waiter approached.

"Yes, certainly, sir," the man answered in careful English. "Is it not, perhaps, Mr. and Misses Gerald?" he smilingly insinuated, offering some cards.

"Miss Gerald," the father corrected him as he took the cards. "Why, hello, Nannie! Here are the Bells! Where are they?" he demanded of the waiter. "Bring them here, and a lot more cups and saucers. Or, hold on! I'd better go myself, Nannie, hadn't I? Of course! You get the crockery, waiter. Where did you say they were?" He bustled up from his chair, without waiting for a distinct reply, and apologized to Lanfear in hurrying away. "You'll excuse me, doctor! I'll be back in half a minute. Friends of ours that came over on the same boat. I must see them, of course, but I don't believe they'll stay. Nannie, don't let Dr. Lanfear get away. I want to have some talk with him. You tell him he'd better come to the Sardegna, here."

Lanfear and Miss Gerald sat a moment in the silence which is apt to follow with young people when they are unexpectedly left to themselves. She kept absently pushing the cards her father had given her up and down on the table between her thumb and forefinger, and Lanfear noted the translucence of her long, thin hand in the sunshine striking across the painted iron surface of the garden movable. The translucence had a pathos for his intelligence which the pensive tilt of her head enhanced. She stopped toying with the cards, and looked at the addresses on them.

"What strange things names are!" she said, as if musing on the fact, with a sigh which he thought disproportioned to the depth of her remark.

"They seem rather irrelevant at times," he admitted, with a smile. "They're mere tags, labels, which can be attached to one as well as another; they seem to belong equally to anybody."

"That is what I always say to myself," she agreed, with more interest than he found explicable.

William Dean Howells

"But finally," he returned, "they're all that's left us, if they're left themselves. They are the only signs to the few who knew us that we ever existed. They stand for our characters, our personality, our mind, our soul."

She said, "That is very true," and then she suddenly gave him the cards. "Do you know these people?"

"I? I thought they were friends of yours," he replied, astonished.

"That is what papa thinks," Miss Gerald said, and while she sat dreamily absent, a rustle of skirts and a flutter of voices pierced from the surrounding shrubbery, and then a lively matron, of as youthful a temperament as the lively girls she brought in her train, burst upon them, and Miss Gerald was passed from one embrace to another until all four had kissed her. She returned their greeting, and shared, in her quieter way, their raptures at their encounter.

"Such a hunt as we've had for you!" the matron shouted. "We've been up-stairs and down-stairs and in my lady's chamber, all over the hotel. Where's your father? Ah, they did get our cards to you!" and by that token Lanfear knew that these ladies were the Bells. He had stood up in a sort of expectancy, but Miss Gerald did not introduce him, and a shadow of embarrassment passed over the party which she seemed to feel least, though he fancied a sort of entreaty in the glance that she let pass over him.

"I suppose he's gone to look for *us*!" Mrs. Bell saved the situation with a protecting laugh. Miss Gerald colored intelligently, and Lanfear could not let Mrs. Bell's implication pass.

"If it is Mrs. Bell," he said, "I can answer that he has. I met you at Magnolia some years ago, Mrs. Bell. Dr. Lanfear."

"Oh, I beg your pardon, Dr. Lanfear," Miss Gerald said. "I couldn't think—"

"Of my tag, my label?" he laughed back. "It isn't very distinctly lettered."

Mrs. Bell was not much minding them jointly. She was singling Lanfear out for the expression of her pleasure in seeing him again, and recalling the incidents of her summer at Magnolia before, it seemed, any of her girls were out. She presented them collectively, and the eldest of them charmingly reminded Lanfear that he had once had the magnanimity to dance with her when she sat, in a little girl's forlorn despair of being danced with, at one of those desolate hops of the good old Osprey House.

"Yes; and now," her mother followed, "we can't wait a moment longer, if we're to get our train for Monte Carlo, girls. We're not going to play, doctor," she made time to explain, "but we are going to look on. Will you tell your father, dear," she said, taking the girl's hands caressingly in hers, and drawing her to her motherly bosom, "that we found you, and did our best to find him? We can't wait now—our carriage is champing the bit at the foot of the stairs—but we're coming back in a week, and then we'll do our best to look you up again." She included Lanfear in her good-bye, and all her girls said good-bye in the same way, and with a whisking of skirts and twitter of voices they vanished through the shrubbery, and faded into the general silence and general sound like a bevy of birds which had swept near and passed by.

Miss Gerald sank quietly into her place, and sat as if nothing had happened, except that she looked a little paler to Lanfear, who remained on foot trying to piece together their interrupted tete-a-tete, but not succeeding, when her father reappeared, red and breathless, and wiping his forehead. "Have they been here, Nannie?" he asked. "I've been following them all over the place, and the *portier* told me just now that he had seen a party of ladies coming down this way."

He got it all out, not so clearly as those women had got everything in, Lanfear reflected, but unmistakably enough as to

William Dean Howells

the fact, and he looked at his daughter as he repeated: "Haven't the Bells been here?"

She shook her head, and said, with her delicate quiet: "Nobody has been here, except—" She glanced at Lanfear, who smiled, but saw no opening for himself in the strange situation. Then she said: "I think I will go and lie down a while, now, papa. I'm rather tired. Good-bye," she said, giving Lanfear her hand; it felt limp and cold; and then she turned to her father again. "Don't you come, papa! I can get back perfectly well by myself. Stay with—"

"I will go with you," her father said, "and if Dr. Lanfear doesn't mind coming—"

"Certainly I will come," Lanfear said, and he passed to the girl's right; she had taken her father's arm; but he wished to offer more support if it were needed. When they had climbed to the open flowery space before the hotel, she seemed aware of the groups of people about. She took her hand from her father's arm, as if unwilling to attract their notice by seeming to need its help, and swept up the gravelled path between him and Lanfear, with her flowing walk.

Her father fell back, as they entered the hotel door, and murmured to Lanfear: "Will you wait till I come down?" ... "I wanted to tell you about my daughter," he explained, when he came back after the quarter of an hour which Lanfear had found rather intense. "It's useless to pretend you wouldn't have noticed—Had nobody been with you after I left you, down there?" He twisted his head in the direction of the pavilion, where they had been breakfasting.

"Yes; Mrs. Bell and her daughters," Lanfear answered, simply.

"Of course! Why do you suppose my daughter denied it?" Mr. Gerald asked.

"I suppose she—had her reasons," Lanfear answered, lamely enough.

"No *reason*, I'm afraid," Mr. Gerald said, and he broke out hopelessly: "She has her mind sound enough, but not—not her memory. She had forgotten that they were there! Are you going to stay in San Remo?" he asked, with an effect of interrupting himself, as if in the wish to put off something, or to make the ground sure before he went on.

"Why," Lanfear said, "I hadn't thought of it. I stopped—I was going to Nice—to test the air for a friend who wishes to bring his invalid wife here, if I approve—but I have just been asking myself why I should go to Nice when I could stay at San Remo. The place takes my fancy. I'm something of an invalid myself—at least I'm on my vacation—and I find a charm in it, if nothing better. Perhaps a charm is enough. It used to be, in primitive medicine."

He was talking to what he felt was not an undivided attention in Mr. Gerald, who said, "I'm glad of it," and then added: "I should like to consult you professionally. I know your reputation in New York—though I'm not a New-Yorker myself—and I don't know any of the doctors here. I suppose I've done rather a wild thing in coming off the way I have, with my daughter; but I felt that I must do something, and I hoped—I felt as if it were getting away from our trouble. It's most fortunate my meeting you, if you can look into the case, and help me out with a nurse, if she's needed, and all that!" To a certain hesitation in Lanfear's face, he added: "Of course, I'm asking your professional help. My name is Abner Gerald— Abner L. Gerald—perhaps you know my standing, and that I'm able to—"

"Oh, it isn't a question of that! I shall be glad to do anything I can," Lanfear said, with a little pang which he tried to keep silent in orienting himself anew towards the girl, whose loveliness he had felt before he had felt her piteousness.

"But before you go further I ought to say that you must have been thinking of my uncle, the first Matthew Lanfear, when you spoke of my reputation; I haven't got any yet; I've only got my uncle's name."

"Oh!" Mr. Gerald said, disappointedly, but after a blank moment he apparently took courage. "You're in the same line, though?"

"If you mean the psychopathic line, without being exactly an alienist, well, yes," Lanfear admitted.

"That's exactly what I mean," the elder said, with renewed hopefulness. "I'm quite willing to risk myself with a man of the same name as Dr. Lanfear. I should like," he said, hurrying on, as if to override any further reluctance of Lanfear's, "to tell you her story, and then—"

"By all means," Lanfear consented, and he put on an air of professionaldeference, while the older man began with a face set for the task.

"It's a long story, or it's a short story, as you choose to make it. We'll make it long, if necessary, later, but now I'll make it short. Five months ago my wife was killed before my daughter's eyes—"

He stopped; Lanfear breathed a gentle "Oh!" and Gerald blurted out:

"Accident—grade crossing—Don't!" he winced at the kindness in Lanfear's eyes, and panted on. "That's over! What happened to *her*—to my daughter—was that she fainted from the shock. When she woke—it was more like a sleep than a swoon—she didn't remember what had happened." Lanfear nodded, with a gravely interested face. "She didn't remember anything that had ever happened before. She knew me, because I was there with her; but she didn't know that she ever had a mother, because she was not there with her. You see?"

"I can imagine," Lanfear assented.

"The whole of her life before the—accident was wiped out as to the facts, as completely as if it had never been; and now every day, every hour, every minute, as it passes, goes with that past. But her faculties—"

"Yes?" Lanfear prompted in the pause which Mr. Gerald made.

"Her intellect—the working powers of her mind, apart from anything like remembering, are as perfect as if she were in full possession of her memory. I believe," the father said, with a pride that had its pathos, "no one can talk with her and not feel that she has a beautiful mind, that she can think better than most girls of her age. She reads, or she lets me read to her, and until it has time to fade, she appreciates it all more fully than I do. At Genoa, where I took her to the palaces for the pictures, I saw that she had kept her feeling for art. When she plays—you will hear her play—it is like composing the music for herself; she does not seem to remember the pieces, she seems to improvise them. You understand?"

Lanfear said that he understood, for he could not disappoint the expectation of the father's boastful love: all that was left him of the ambitions he must once have had for his child.

The poor, little, stout, unpicturesque elderly man got up and began to walk to and fro in the room which he had turned into with Lanfear, and to say, more to himself than to Lanfear, as if balancing one thing against another: "The merciful thing is that she has been saved from the horror and the sorrow. She knows no more of either than she knows of her mother's love for her. They were very much alike in looks and mind, and they were always together more like persons of the same age— sisters, or girl friends; but she has lost all knowledge of that, as of other things. And then there is the question whether she won't some time, sooner or later, come into both the horror and the sorrow." He stopped and looked at Lanfear. "She has these sudden fits of drowsiness, when she *must* sleep; and I never see her wake from them without being afraid that she has wakened to everything—that she has got back into her full self, and taken up the terrible burden that my old shoulders are used to. What do you think?"

Lanfear felt the appeal so keenly that in the effort to answer faithfully he was aware of being harsher than he meant. "That is a chance we can't forecast. But it is a chance. The fact that the drowsiness recurs periodically—"

"It doesn't," the father pleaded. "We don't know when it will come on."

"It scarcely matters. The periodicity wouldn't affect the possible result which you dread. I don't say that it is probable. But it's one of the possibilities. It has," Lanfear added, "its logic."

"Ah, its logic!"

"Its logic, yes. My business, of course, would be to restore her to health at any risk. So far as her mind is affected—"

"Her mind is not affected!" the father retorted.

"I beg your pardon—her memory—it might be restored with her physical health. You understand that? It is a chance; it might or it might not happen."

The father was apparently facing a risk which he had not squarely faced before. "I suppose so," he faltered. After a moment he added, with more courage: "You must do the best you can, at any risk."

Lanfear rose, too. He said, with returning kindness in his tones, if not his words: "I should like to study the case, Mr. Gerald. It's very interesting, and—and—if you'll forgive me— very touching."

"Thank you."

"If you decide to stay in San Remo, I will—Do you suppose I could get a room in this hotel? I don't like mine."

"Why, I haven't any doubt you can. Shall we ask?"

# III

It was from the Hotel Sardegna that Lanfear satisfied his conscience by pushing his search for climate on behalf of his friend's neurasthenic wife. He decided that Ospedaletti, with a milder air and more sheltered seat in its valley of palms, would be better for her than San Remo. He wrote his friend to that effect, and then there was no preoccupation to hinder him in his devotion to the case of Miss Gerald. He put the case first in the order of interest rather purposely, and even with a sense of effort, though he could not deny to himself that a like case related to a different personality might have been less absorbing. But he tried to keep his scientific duty to it pure of that certain painful pleasure which, as a young man not much over thirty, he must feel in the strange affliction of a young and beautiful girl.

Though there was no present question of medicine, he could be installed near her, as the friend that her father insisted upon making him, without contravention of the social formalities. His care of her hardly differed from that of her father, except that it involved a closer and more premeditated study. They did not try to keep her from the sort of association which, in a large hotel of the type of the Sardegna, entails no sort of obligation to intimacy. They sat together at the long table, midway of the dining-room, which maintained the tradition of the old table-d'hote against the small tables ranged along the walls. Gerald had an amiable old man's liking for talk, and Lanfear saw that he willingly escaped, among their changing companions, from the pressure of his anxieties. He left his daughter very much to Lanfear, during these excursions, but Lanfear was far from meaning to keep her to himself. He thought it better that she should follow her father in his forays among their neighbors, and he encouraged her to continue such talk with them as she might be brought into. He tried to guard her future encounters with them, so that she should not show more than a young girl's usual diffidence at a second meeting; and in the frequent substitution of one presence for another across the table, she was fairly safe.

A natural light-heartedness, of which he had glimpses from the first, returned to her. One night, at the dance given by some of the guests to some others, she went through the gayety in joyous triumph. She danced mostly with Lanfear, but she had other partners, and she won a pleasing popularity by the American quality of her waltzing. Lanfear had already noted that her forgetfulness was not always so constant or so inclusive as her father had taught him to expect; Mr. Gerald's statement had been the large, general fact from which there was sometimes a shrinking in the particulars. While the warmth of an agreeable experience lasted, her mind kept record of it, slight or full; if the experience were unpleasant the memory was more apt to fade at once. After that dance she repeated to her father the little compliments paid her, and told him, laughing, they were to reward him for sitting up so late as her chaperon. Emotions persisted in her consciousness as the tremor lasts in a smitten cord, but events left little trace. She retained a sense of personalities; she was lastingly sensible of temperaments; but names were nothing to her. She could not tell her father who had said the nice things to her, and their joint study of her dancing-card did not help them out.

Her relation to Lanfear, though it might be a subject of international scrutiny, was hardly a subject of censure. He was known as Dr. Lanfear, but he was not at first known as her physician; he was conjectured her cousin or something like that; he might even be her betrothed in the peculiar American arrangement of such affairs. Personally people saw in him a serious-looking young man, better dressed and better mannered than they thought most Americans, and unquestionably handsomer, with his Spanish skin and eyes, and his brown beard of the Vandyke cut which was then already beginning to be rather belated.

Other Americans in the hotel were few and transitory; and if the English had any mind about Miss Gerald different from their mind about other girls, it would be perhaps to the effect that she was quite mad; by this they would mean that she was a little odd; but for the rest they had apparently no mind about her. With the help of one of the English ladies her father had replaced the homesick Irish maid whom he had sent back to New York from Genoa, with an Italian, and in the shelter of her gay affection and ignorant sympathy Miss Gerald had a security supplemented by the easy social environment. If she did not look very well, she did not differ from most other American women in that; and if she seemed to confide herself more severely to the safe-keeping of her physician, that was the way of all women patients.

Whether the Bells found the spectacle of depravity at Monte Carlo more attractive than the smiling face of nature at San Remo or not, they did not return, but sent for their baggage from their hotel, and were not seen again by the Geralds. Lanfear's friend with the invalid wife wrote from Ospedaletti, with apologies which inculpated him for the disappointment, that she had found the air impossible in a single day, and they were off for Cannes. Lanfear and the Geralds, therefore, continued together in the hotel without fear or obligation to others, and in an immunity in which their right to breakfast exclusively in that pavilion on the garden wall was almost explicitly conceded. No one, after a few mornings of tacit possession, would have disputed their claim, and there, day after day, in the mild monotony of the December sunshine, they sat and drank their coffee, and talked of the sights which the peasants in the street, and the tourists in the promenade beyond it, afforded. The rows of stumpy palms which separated the road from the walk were not so high but that they had the whole lift of the sea to the horizon where it lost itself in a sky that curved blue as turquoise to the zenith overhead. The sun rose from its morning bath on the left, and sank to its evening bath on the right, and in making its climb of the spacious arc between, shed a heat as great as that of summer, but not the heat of summer, on the pretty world of villas and hotels, towered over by the olive-gray slopes of the pine-clad heights behind and above them. From these tops a fine, keen cold fell with the waning afternoon, which sharpened through the sunset till the dusk; but in the morning the change was from the chill to the glow, and they could sit in their pavilion, under the willowy droop of the eucalyptus-trees which have brought the Southern Pacific to the Riviera, with increasing comfort.

In the restlessness of an elderly man, Gerald sometimes left the young people to their intolerable delays over their coffee, and walked off into the little stone and stucco city below, or went and sat with his cigar on one of the benches under the palm-lined promenade, which the pale northern consumptives shared with the swarthy peasant girls resting from their burdens, and the wrinkled grandmothers of their race passively or actively begging from the strangers.

While she kept her father in sight it seemed that Miss Gerald could maintain her hold of his identity, and one morning she said, with the tender fondness for him which touched Lanfear: "When he sits there among those sick people and poor people, then he knows they are in the world."

She turned with a question graver in her look than usual, and he said: "Yes, we might help them oftener if we could remember that their misery was going on all the time, like some great natural process, day or dark, heat or cold, which seems to stop when we stop thinking of it. Nothing, for us, at least, exists unless it is recalled to us."

"Yes," she said, in her turn, "I have noticed that. But don't you sometimes—sometimes"—she knit her forehead, as if to keep her thought from escaping—"have a feeling as if what you were doing, or saying, or seeing, had all happened before, just as it is now?"

"Oh yes; that occurs to every one."

"But don't you—don't you have hints of things, of ideas, as if you had known them, in some previous existence—"

William Dean Howells

She stopped, and Lanfear recognized, with a kind of impatience, the experience which young people make much of when they have it, and sometimes pretend to when they have merely heard of it. But there could be no pose or pretence in her. He smilingly suggested:

"'For something is, or something seems,
Like glimpses of forgotten dreams.'

These weird impressions are no more than that, probably."

"Ah, I don't believe it," the girl said. "They are too real for that. They come too often, and they make me feel as if they would come more fully, some time. If there was a life before this—do you believe there was?—they may be things that happened there. Or they may be things that will happen in a life after this. You believe in *that*, don't you?"

"In a life after this, or their happening in it?"

"Well, both."

Lanfear evaded her, partly. "They could be premonitions, prophecies, of a future life, as easily as fragmentary records of a past life. I suppose we do not begin to be immortal merely after death."

"No." She lingered out the word in dreamy absence, as if what they had been saying had already passed from her thought.

"But, Miss Gerald," Lanfear ventured, "have these impressions of yours grown more definite—fuller, as you say—of late?"

"My impressions?" She frowned at him, as if the look of interest, more intense than usual in his eyes, annoyed her. "I don't know what you mean."

Lanfear felt bound to follow up her lead, whether she wished it or not. "A good third of our lives here is passed in sleep. I'm not always sure that we are right in treating the mental—for certainly they are mental—experiences of that time as altogether trivial, or insignificant."

She seemed to understand now, and she protested: "But I don't mean dreams. I mean things that really happened, or that really will happen."

"Like something you can give me an instance of? Are they painful things, or pleasant, mostly?"

She hesitated. "They are things that you know happen to other people, but you can't believe would ever happen to you."

"Do they come when you are just drowsing, or just waking from a drowse?"

"They are not dreams," she said, almost with vexation.

"Yes, yes, I understand," he hesitated to retrieve himself. "But *I* have had floating illusions, just before I fell asleep, or when I was sensible of not being quite awake, which seemed to differ from dreams. They were not so dramatic, but they were more pictorial; they were more visual than the things in dreams."

"Yes," she assented. "They are something like that. But I should not call them illusions."

"No. And they represent scenes, events?"

"You said yourself they were not dramatic."

"I meant, represent pictorially."

"No; they are like the landscape that flies back from your train or towards it. I can't explain it," she ended, rising with what he felt a displeasure in his pursuit.

William Dean Howells

# IV

He reported what had passed to her father when Mr. Gerald came back from his stroll into the town, with his hands full of English papers; Gerald had even found a New York paper at the news-stand; and he listened with an apparent postponement of interest.

"I think," Lanfear said, "that she has some shadowy recollection, or rather that the facts come to her in a jarred, confused way—the elements of pictures, not pictures. But I am afraid that my inquiry has offended her."

"I guess not," Gerald said, dryly, as if annoyed. "What makes you think so?"

"Merely her manner. And I don't know that anything is to be gained by such an inquiry."

"Perhaps not," Gerald allowed, with an inattention which vexed Lanfear in his turn.

The elderly man looked up, from where he sat provisionally in the hotel veranda, into Lanfear's face; Lanfear had remained standing. "*I* don't believe she's offended. Or she won't be long. One thing, she'll forget it."

He was right enough, apparently. Miss Gerald came out of the hotel door towards them, smiling equally for both, with the indefinable difference between cognition and recognition habitual in her look. She was dressed for a walk, and she seemed to expect them to go with her. She beamed gently upon Lanfear; there was no trace of umbrage in her sunny gayety. Her face had, as always, its lurking pathos, but in its appeal to Lanfear now there were only trust and the wish of pleasing him.

They started side by side for their walk, while her father drove beside them in one of the little public carriages, mounting to the Berigo Road, through a street of the older San Remo, and issuing on a bare little piazza looking towards the walls and roofs of the mediaeval city, clustered together like cliff-dwellings, and down on the gardens that fell from the villas and the hotels. A parapet kept the path on the roadside nearest the declivities, and from point to point benches were put for the convenient enjoyment of the prospect. Mr. Gerald preferred to take his pleasure from the greater elevation of the seat in his victoria; his daughter and Lanfear leaned on the wall, and looked up to the sky and out to the sea, both of the same blue.

The palms and eucalyptus-trees darkened about the villas; the bits of vineyard, in their lingering crimson or lingering gold, and the orchards of peaches and persimmons enriched with the varying reds of their ripening leaves and fruits the enchanting color scheme. The rose and geranium hedges were in bloom; the feathery green of the pepper-trees was warmed by the red-purple of their grape-like clusters of blossoms; the perfume of lemon flowers wandered vaguely upwards from some point which they could not fix.

Nothing of all the beauty seemed lost upon the girl, so bereft that she could enjoy no part of it from association. Lanfear observed that she was not fatigued by any such effort as he was always helplessly making to match what he saw with something he had seen before. Now, when this effort betrayed itself, she said, smiling: "How strange it is that you see things for what they are like, and not for what they are!"

"Yes, it's a defect, I'm afraid, sometimes. Perhaps—"

"Perhaps what?" she prompted him in the pause he made.

"Nothing. I was wondering whether in some other possible life our consciousness would not be more independent of what we have been than it seems to be here." She looked askingly at him. "I mean whether there shall not be something absolute in

William Dean Howells

our existence, whether it shall not realize itself more in each experience of the moment, and not be always seeking to verify itself from the past."

"Isn't that what you think is the way with me already?" She turned upon him smiling, and he perceived that in her New York version of a Parisian costume, with her lace hat of summer make and texture and the vivid parasol she twirled upon her shoulder, she was not only a very pretty girl, but a fashionable one. There was something touching in the fact, and a little bewildering. To the pretty girl, the fashionable girl, he could have answered with a joke, but the stricken intelligence had a claim to his seriousness. Now, especially, he noted what had from time to time urged itself upon his perception. If the broken ties which once bound her to the past were beginning to knit again, her recovery otherwise was not apparent. As she stood there her beauty had signally the distinction of fragility, the delicacy of shattered nerves in which there was yet no visible return to strength. A feeling, which had intimated itself before, a sense as of being in the presence of a disembodied spirit, possessed him, and brought, in its contradiction of an accepted theory, a suggestion that was destined to become conviction. He had always said to himself that there could be no persistence of personality, of character, of identity, of consciousness, except through memory; yet here, to the last implication of temperament, they all persisted. The soul that was passing in its integrity through time without the helps, the crutches, of remembrance by which his own personality supported itself, why should not it pass so through eternity without that loss of identity which was equivalent to annihilation?

Her waiting eyes recalled him from his inquiry, and with an effort he answered, "Yes, I think you do have your being here and now, Miss Gerald, to an unusual degree."

"And you don't think that is wrong?"

"Wrong? Why? How?"

"Oh, I don't know." She looked round, and her eye fell upon her father waiting for them in his carriage beside the walk. The sight supplied her with the notion which Lanfear perceived would not have occurred otherwise. "Then why doesn't papa want me to remember things?"

"I don't know," Lanfear temporized. "Doesn't he?"

"I can't always tell. Should—should *you* wish me to remember more than I do?"

"I?"

She looked at him with entreaty. "Do you think it would make my father happier if I did?"

"That I can't say," Lanfear answered. "People are often the sadder for what they remember. If I were your father—Excuse me! I don't mean anything so absurd. But in his place—"

He stopped, and she said, as if she were satisfied with his broken reply: "It is very curious. When I look at him—when I am with him—I know him; but when he is away, I don't remember him." She seemed rather interested in the fact than distressed by it; she even smiled.

"And me," he ventured, "is it the same with regard to me?"

She did not say; she asked, smiling: "Do you remember me when I am away?"

"Yes!" he answered. "As perfectly as if you were with me. I can see you, hear you, feel the touch of your hand, your dress— Good heavens!" he added to himself under his breath. "What am I saying to this poor child!"

In the instinct of escaping from himself he started forward, and she moved with him. Mr. Gerald's watchful driver followed them with the carriage.

William Dean Howells

"That is very strange," she said, lightly. "Is it so with you about everyone?"

"No," he replied, briefly, almost harshly. He asked, abruptly: "Miss Gerald, are there any times when you know people in their absence?"

"Just after I wake from a nap—yes. But it doesn't last. That is, it seems to me it doesn't. I'm not sure."

As they followed the winding of the pleasant way, with the villas on the slopes above and on the slopes below, she began to talk of them, and to come into that knowledge of each which formed her remembrance of them from former knowledge of them, but which he knew would fade when she passed them.

The next morning, when she came down unwontedly late to breakfast in their pavilion, she called gayly:

"Dr. Lanfear! It *is* Dr. Lanfear?"

"I should be sorry if it were not, since you seem to expect it, Miss Gerald."

"Oh, I just wanted to be sure. Hasn't my father been here, yet?" It was the first time she had shown herself aware of her father except in his presence, as it was the first time she had named Lanfear to his face.

He suppressed a remote stir of anxiety, and answered: "He went to get his newspapers; he wished you not to wait. I hope you slept well?"

"Splendidly. But I was very tired last night; I don't know why, exactly."

"We had rather a long walk."

"Did we have a walk yesterday?"

"Yes."

"Then it was *so*! I thought I had dreamed it. I was beginning to remember something, and my father asked me what it was, and then I couldn't remember. Do you believe I shall keep on remembering?"

"I don't see why you shouldn't."

"Should you wish me to?" she asked, in evident, however unconscious, recurrence to their talk of the day before.

"Why not?"

She sighed. "I don't know. If it's like some of those dreams or gleams. Is remembering pleasant?"

Lanfear thought for a moment. Then he said, in the honesty he thought best to use with her: "For the most part I should say it was painful. Life is tolerable enough while it passes, but when it is past, what remains seems mostly to hurt and humiliate. I don't know why we should remember so insistently the foolish things and wrong things we do, and not recall the times when we acted, without an effort, wisely and rightly." He thought he had gone too far, and he hedged a little. "I don't mean that we *can't* recall those times. We can and do, to console and encourage ourselves; but they don't recur, without our willing, as the others do."

She had poured herself a cup of coffee, and she played with the spoon in her saucer while she seemed to listen. But she could not have been listening, for when she put down her spoon and leaned back in her chair, she said: "In those dreams the things come from such a very far way back, and they don't belong to a life that is like this. They belong to a life like what you hear the life after this is. We are the same as we are here; but the things are different. We haven't the same rules, the same

William Dean Howells

wishes—I can't explain."

"You mean that we are differently conditioned?"

"Yes. And if you can understand, I feel as if I remembered long back of this, and long forward of this. But one can't remember forward!"

"That wouldn't be remembrance; no, it would be prescience; and your consciousness here, as you were saying yesterday, is through knowing, not remembering."

She stared at him. "Was that yesterday? I thought it was—to-morrow." She rubbed her hand across her forehead as people do when they wish to clear their minds. Then she sighed deeply. "It tires me so. And yet I can't help trying." A light broke over her face at the sound of a step on the gravel walk near by, and she said, laughing, without looking round: "That is papa! I knew it was his step."

# V

Such return of memory as she now had was like memory in what we call the lower lives. It increased, fluctuantly, with an ebb in which it almost disappeared, but with a flow that in its advance carried it beyond its last flood-tide mark. After the first triumph in which she could address Lanfear by his name, and could greet her father as her father, there were lapses in which she knew them as before, without naming them. Except mechanically to repeat the names of other people when reminded of them, she did not pass beyond cognition to recognition. Events still left no trace upon her; or if they did she was not sure whether they were things she had dreamed or experienced. But her memory grew stronger in the region where the bird knows its way home to the nest, or the bee to the hive. She had an unerring instinct for places where she had once been, and she found her way to them again without the help from the association which sometimes failed Lanfear. Their walks were always taken with her father's company in his carriage, but they sometimes left him at a point of the Berigo Road, and after a long detour among the vineyards and olive orchards of the heights above, rejoined him at another point they had agreed upon with him. One afternoon, when Lanfear had climbed the rough pave of the footways with her to one of the summits, they stopped to rest on the wall of a terrace, where they sat watching the changing light on the sea, through a break in the trees. The shadows surprised them on their height, and they had to make their way among them over the farm paths and by the dry beds of the torrents to the carriage road far below. They had been that walk only once before, and Lanfear failed of his reckoning, except the downward course which must bring them out on the high-road at last. But Miss Gerald's instinct saved them where his reason failed. She did not remember, but she knew the way, and she led him on as if she were inventing it, or as if it had been indelibly traced upon her mind and she had only to follow the mystical lines within to be sure of her course. She confessed to being very tired, and each step must have increased her fatigue, but each step seemed to clear her perception of the next to be taken.

Suddenly, when Lanfear was blaming himself for bringing all this upon her, and then for trusting to her guidance, he recognized a certain peasant's house, and in a few moments they had descended the olive-orchard terraces to a broken cistern in the clear twilight beyond the dusk. She suddenly halted him. "There, there! It happened then—now—this instant!"

"What?"

"That feeling of being here before! There is the curb of the old cistern; and the place where the terrace wall is broken; and the path up to the vineyard—Don't you feel it, too?" she demanded, with a joyousness which had no pleasure for him.

"Yes, certainly. We were here last week. We went up the path to the farm-house to get some water."

"Yes, now I am remembering—remembering!" She stood with eagerly parted lips, and glancing quickly round with glowing eyes, whose light faded in the same instant. "No!" she said, mournfully, "it's gone."

A sound of wheels in the road ceased, and her father's voice called: "Don't you want to take my place, and let me walk awhile, Nannie?"

"No. You come to me, papa. Something very strange has happened; something you will be surprised at. Hurry!" She seemed to be joking, as he was, while she beckoned him impatiently towards her.

He had left his carriage, and he came up with a heavy man's quickened pace. "Well, what is the wonderful thing?" he panted out.

She stared blankly at him, without replying, and they silently made their way to Mr. Gerald's carriage.

"I lost the way, and Miss Gerald found it," Lanfear explained, as he helped her to the place beside her father.

She said nothing, and almost with sinking into the seat, she sank into that deep slumber which from time to time overtook her.

"I didn't know we had gone so far—or rather that we had waited so long before we started down the hills," Lanfear apologized in an involuntary whisper.

"Oh, it's all right," her father said, trying to adjust the girl's fallen head to his shoulder. "Get in and help me—"

Lanfear obeyed, and lent a physician's skilled aid, which left the cumbrous efforts of her father to the blame he freely bestowed on them. "You'll have to come here on the other side," he said. "There's room enough for all three. Or, hold on! Let me take your place." He took the place in front, and left her to Lanfear's care, with the trust which was the physician's right, and with a sense of the girl's dependence in which she was still a child to him.

They did not speak till well on the way home. Then the father leaned forward and whispered huskily: "Do you think she's as strong as she was?"

Lanfear waited, as if thinking the facts over. He murmured back: "No. She's better. She's not so strong."

"Yes," the father murmured. "I understand."

What Gerald understood by Lanfear's words might not have been their meaning, but what Lanfear meant was that there was now an interfusion of the past and present in her daily experience. She still did not remember, but she had moments in which she hovered upon such knowledge of what had

William Dean Howells

happened as she had of actual events. When she was stronger she seemed farther from this knowledge; when she was weaker she was nearer it. So it seemed to him in that region where he could be sure of his own duty when he looked upon it singly as concern for her health. No inquiry for the psychological possibilities must be suffered to divide his effort for her physical recovery, though there might come with this a cessation of the timeless dream-state in which she had her being, and she might sharply realize the past, as the anaesthete realizes his return to agony from insensibility. The quality of her mind was as different from the thing called culture as her manner from convention. A simplicity beyond the simplicity of childhood was one with a poetic color in her absolute ideas. But this must cease with her restoration to the strength in which she could alone come into full and clear self-consciousness. So far as Lanfear could give reality to his occupation with her disability, he was ministering to a mind diseased; not to "rase out its written trouble," but if possible to restore the obliterated record, and enable her to spell its tragic characters. If he could, he would have shrunk from this office; but all the more because he specially had to do with the mystical side of medicine, he always tried to keep his relation to her free from personal feeling, and his aim single and matter-of-fact.

It was hard to do this; and there was a glamour in the very topographical and meteorological environment. The autumn was a long delight in which the constant sea, the constant sky, knew almost as little variance as the unchanging Alps. The days passed in a procession of sunny splendor, neither hot nor cold, nor of the temper of any determinate season, unless it were an abiding spring-time. The flowers bloomed, and the grass kept green in a reverie of May. But one afternoon of January, while Lanfear was going about in a thin coat and panama hat, a soft, fresh wind began to blow from the east. It increased till sunset, and then fell. In the morning he looked out on a world in which the spring had stiffened overnight into winter. A thick frost painted the leaves and flowers; icicles hung from pipes and vents; the frozen streams flashed back from their arrested flow the sun as it shone from the cold heaven, and blighted and blackened the hedges of geranium and rose, the borders of heliotrope, the fields of pinks. The leaves of the bananas hung limp about their stems; the palms rattled like skeletons in the wind when it began to blow again over the shrunken landscape.

William Dean Howells

# VI

The caprice of a climate which vaunted itself perpetual summer was a godsend to all the strangers strong enough to bear it without suffering. For the sick an indoor life of huddling about the ineffectual fires of the south began, and lasted for the fortnight that elapsed before the Riviera got back its advertised temperature. Miss Gerald had drooped in the milder weather; but the cold braced and lifted her, and with its help she now pushed her walks farther, and was eager every day for some excursion to the little towns that whitened along the shores, or the villages that glimmered from the olive-orchards of the hills. Once she said to Lanfear, when they were climbing through the brisk, clear air: "It seems to me as if I had been here before. Have I?"

"No. This is the first time."

She said no more, but seemed disappointed in his answer, and he suggested: "Perhaps it is the cold that reminds you of our winters at home, and makes you feel that the scene is familiar."

"Yes, that is it!" she returned, joyously. "Was there snow, there, like that on the mountains yonder?"

"A good deal more, I fancy. That will be gone in a few days, and at home, you know, our snow lasts for weeks."

"Then that is what I was thinking of," she said, and she ran strongly and lightly forward. "Come!"

When the harsh weather passed and the mild climate returned there was no lapse of her strength. A bloom, palely pink as the flowers that began to flush the almond-trees, came upon her delicate beauty, a light like that of the lengthening days dawned in her eyes. She had an instinct for the earliest violets among the grass under the olives; she was first to hear the blackcaps singing in the garden-tops; and nothing that was novel in her experience seemed alien to it. This was the sum of what Lanfear got by the questioning which he needlessly tried to keep indirect. She knew that she was his patient, and in what manner, and she had let him divine that her loss of memory was suffering as well as deprivation. She had not merely the fatigue which we all undergo from the effort to recall things, and which sometimes reaches exhaustion; but there was apparently in the void of her oblivion a perpetual rumor of events, names, sensations, like—Lanfear felt that he inadequately conjectured—the subjective noises which are always in the ears of the deaf. Sometimes, in the distress of it, she turned to him for help, and when he was able to guess what she was striving for, a radiant relief and gratitude transfigured her face. But this could not last, and he learned to note how soon the stress and tension of her effort returned. His compassion for her at such times involved a temptation, or rather a question, which he had to silence by a direct effort of his will. Would it be worse, would it be greater anguish for her to know at once the past that now tormented her consciousness with its broken and meaningless reverberations? Then he realized that it was impossible to help her even through the hazard of telling her what had befallen; that no such effect as was to be desired could be anticipated from the outside.

If he turned to her father for counsel or instruction, or even a participation in his responsibility, he was met by an optimistic patience which exasperated him, if it did not complicate the case. Once, when Lanfear forbearingly tried to share with him his anxiety for the effect of a successful event, he was formed to be outright, and remind him, in so many words, that the girl's restoration might be through anguish which he could not measure.

Gerald faltered aghast; then he said: "It mustn't come to that; you mustn't let it."

"How do you expect me to prevent it?" Lanfear demanded, in his vexation.

William Dean Howells

Gerald caught his breath. "If she gets well, she will remember?"

"I don't say that. It seems probable. Do you wish her being to remain bereft of one-half its powers?"

"Oh, how do I know what I want?" the poor man groaned. "I only know that I trust you entirely, Doctor Lanfear. Whatever you think best will be best and wisest, no matter what the outcome is."

He got away from Lanfear with these hopeless words, and again Lanfear perceived that the case was left wholly to him. His consolation was the charm of the girl's companionship, the delight of a nature knowing itself from moment to moment as if newly created. For her, as nearly as he could put the fact into words, the actual moment contained the past and the future as well as the present. When he saw in her the persistence of an exquisite personality independent of the means by which he realized his own continuous identity, he sometimes felt as if in the presence of some angel so long freed from earthly allegiance that it had left all record behind, as we leave here the records of our first years. If an echo of the past reached her, it was apt to be trivial and insignificant, like those unimportant experiences of our remotest childhood, which remain to us from a world outlived.

It was not an insipid perfection of character which reported itself in these celestial terms, and Lanfear conjectured that angelic immortality, if such a thing were, could not imply perfection except at the cost of one-half of human character. When the girl wore a dress that she saw pleased him more than another, there was a responsive pleasure in her eyes, which he could have called vanity if he would; and she had at times a wilfulness which he could have accused of being obstinacy. She showed a certain jealousy of any experiences of his apart from her own, not because they included others, but because they excluded her. He was aware of an involuntary vigilance in her, which could not leave his motives any more than his actions unsearched. But in her conditioning she could not repent; she could only offer him at some other time the unconscious reparation of her obedience. The self-criticism which the child has not learned she had forgotten, but in her oblivion the wish to please existed as perfectly as in the ignorance of childhood.

This, so far as he could ever put into words, was the interior of the world where he dwelt apart with her. Its exterior continued very like that of other worlds where two young people have their being. Now and then a more transitory guest at the Grand Hotel Sardegna perhaps fancied it the iridescent orb which takes the color of the morning sky, and is destined, in the course of nature, to the danger of collapse in which planetary space abounds. Some rumor of this could not fail to reach Lanfear, but he ignored it as best he could in always speaking gravely of Miss Gerald as his patient, and authoritatively treating her as such. He convinced some of these witnesses against their senses; for the others, he felt that it mattered little what they thought, since, if it reached her, it could not pierce her isolation for more than the instant in which the impression from absent things remained to her.

A more positive embarrassment, of a kind Lanfear was not prepared for, beset him in an incident which would have been more touching if he had been less singly concerned for the girl. A pretty English boy, with the dawn of a peachy bloom on his young cheeks, and an impulsiveness commoner with English youth than our own, talked with Miss Gerald one evening and the next day sent her an armful of flowers with his card. He followed this attention with a call at her father's apartment, and after Miss Gerald seemed to know him, and they had, as he told Lanfear, a delightful time together, she took up his card from the table where it was lying, and asked him if he could tell her who that gentleman was. The poor fellow's inference was that she was making fun of him, and he came to Lanfear, as an obvious friend of the family, for an explanation. He reported the incident, with indignant tears standing in his eyes: "What did she mean by it? If she took my flowers, she must have known that—that—they—And to pretend to forget my name! Oh, I say, it's too bad! She could have got rid of me

William Dean Howells

without that. Girls have ways enough, you know."

"Yes, yes," Lanfear assented, slowly, to gain time. "I can assure you that Miss Gerald didn't mean anything that could wound you. She isn't very well—she's rather odd—"

"Do you mean that she's out of her mind? She can talk as well as any one—better!"

"No, not that. But she's often in pain—greatly in pain when she can't recall a name, and I've no doubt she was trying to recall yours with the help of your card. She would be the last in the world to be indifferent to your feelings. I imagine she scarcely knew what she was doing at the moment."

"Then, do you think—do you suppose—it would be any good my trying to see her again? If she wouldn't be indifferent to my feelings, do you think there would be any hope—Really, you know, I would give anything to believe that my feelings wouldn't offend her. You understand me?"

"Perhaps I do."

"I've never met a more charming girl and—she isn't engaged, is she? She isn't engaged to you? I don't mean to press the question, but it's a question of life and death with me, you know."

Lanfear thought he saw his way out of the coil. "I can tell you, quite as frankly as you ask, that Miss Gerald isn't engaged to *me*."

"Then it's somebody else—somebody in America! Well, I hope she'll be happy; *I* never shall." He offered his hand to Lanfear. "I'm off."

"Oh, here's the doctor, now," a voice said behind them where they stood by the garden wall, and they turned to confront Gerald with his daughter.

"Why! Are you going?" she said to the Englishman, and she put out her hand to him.

"Yes, Mr. Evers is going." Lanfear came to the rescue.

"Oh, I'm sorry," the girl said, and the youth responded.

"That's very good of you. I—good-by! I hope you'll be very happy—I—" He turned abruptly away, and ran into the hotel.

"What has he been crying for?" Miss Gerald asked, turning from a long look after him.

Lanfear did not know quite what to say; but he hazarded saying: "He was hurt that you had forgotten him when he came to see you this afternoon."

"Did he come to see me?" she asked; and Lanfear exchanged looks of anxiety, pain, and reassurance with her father. "I am so sorry. Shall I go after him and tell him?"

"No; I explained; he's all right," Lanfear said.

"You want to be careful, Nannie," her father added, "about people's feelings when you meet them, and afterwards seem not to know them."

"But I *do* know them, papa," she remonstrated.

"You want to be careful," her father repeated.

"I will—I will, indeed." Her lips quivered, and the tears came, which Lanfear had to keep from flowing by what quick turn he could give to something else.

An obscure sense of the painful incident must have lingered with her after its memory had perished. One afternoon when Lanfear and her father went with her to the military concert in the sycamore-planted piazza near the Vacherie Suisse, where

William Dean Howells

they often came for a cup of tea, she startled them by bowing gayly to a young lieutenant of engineers standing there with some other officers, and making the most of the prospect of pretty foreigners which the place afforded. The lieutenant returned the bow with interest, and his eyes did not leave their party as long as they remained. Within the bounds of deference for her, it was evident that his comrades were joking about the honor done him by this charming girl. When the Geralds started homeward Lanfear was aware of a trio of officers following them, not conspicuously, but unmistakably; and after that, he could not start on his walks with Miss Gerald and her father without the sense that the young lieutenant was hovering somewhere in their path, waiting in the hopes of another bow from her. The officer was apparently not discouraged by his failure to win recognition from her, and what was amounting to annoyance for Lanfear reached the point where he felt he must share it with her father. He had nearly as much trouble in imparting it to him as he might have had with Miss Gerald herself. He managed, but when he required her father to put a stop to it he perceived that Gerald was as helpless as she would have been. He first wished to verify the fact from its beginning with her, but this was not easy.

"Nannie," he said, "why did you bow to that officer the other day?"

"What officer, papa? When?"

"You know; there by the band-stand, at the Swiss Dairy."

She stared blankly at him, and it was clear that it was all as if it had not been with her. He insisted, and then she said: "Perhaps I thought I knew him, and was afraid I should hurt his feelings if I didn't recognize him. But I don't remember it at all." The curves of her mouth drooped, and her eyes grieved, so that her father had not the heart to say more. She left them, and when he was alone with Lanfear he said:

"You see how it is!"

"Yes, I saw how it was before. But what do you wish to do?"

"Do you mean that he will keep it up?"

"Decidedly, he'll keep it up. He has every right to from his point of view."

"Oh, well, then, my dear fellow, you must stop it, somehow. You'll know how to do it."

"I?" said Lanfear, indignantly; but his vexation was not so great that he did not feel a certain pleasure in fulfilling this strangest part of his professional duty, when at the beginning of their next excursion he put Miss Gerald into the victoria with her father and fell back to the point at which he had seen the lieutenant waiting to haunt their farther progress. He put himself plumply in front of the officer and demanded in very blunt Italian: "What do you want?"

The lieutenant stared him over with potential offence, in which his delicately pencilled mustache took the shape of a light sneer, and demanded in his turn, in English much better than Lanfear's Italian: "What right have you to ask?"

"The right of Miss Gerald's physician. She is an invalid in my charge."

A change quite indefinable except as the visible transition from coxcomb to gentleman passed over the young lieutenant's comely face. "An invalid?" he faltered.

"Yes," Lanfear began; and then, with a rush of confidence which the change in the officer's face justified, "one very strangely, very tragically afflicted. Since she saw her mother killed in an accident a year ago she remembers nothing. She bowed to you because she saw you looking at her, and supposed you must be an acquaintance. May I assure you that you are altogether mistaken?"

The lieutenant brought his heels together, and bent low. "I beg her pardon with all my heart. I am very, very sorry. I will do anything I can. I would like to stop that. May I bring my mother to call on Miss Gerald?"

He offered his hand, and Lanfear wrung it hard, a lump of gratitude in his throat choking any particular utterance, while a fine shame for his late hostile intention covered him.

When the lieutenant came, with all possible circumstance, bringing the countess, his mother, Mr. Gerald overwhelmed them with hospitality of every form. The Italian lady responded effusively, and more sincerely cooed and murmured her compassionate interest in his daughter. Then all parted the best of friends; but when it was over, Miss Gerald did not know what it had been about. She had not remembered the lieutenant or her father's vexation, or any phase of the incident which was now closed. Nothing remained of it but the lieutenant's right, which he gravely exercised, of saluting them respectfully whenever he met them.

# VII

Earlier, Lanfear had never allowed himself to be far out of call from Miss Gerald's father, especially during the daytime slumbers into which she fell, and from which they both always dreaded her awakening. But as the days went on and the event continued the same he allowed himself greater range. Formerly the three went their walks or drives together, but now he sometimes went alone. In these absences he found relief from the stress of his constant vigilance; he was able to cast off the bond which enslaves the physician to his patient, and which he must ignore at times for mere self-preservation's sake; but there was always a lurking anxiety, which, though he refused to let it define itself to him, shortened the time and space he tried to put between them.

One afternoon in April, when he left her sleeping, he was aware of somewhat recklessly placing himself out of reach in a lonely excursion to a village demolished by the earthquake of 1887, and abandoned himself, in the impressions and incidents of his visit to the ruin, to a luxury of impersonal melancholy which the physician cannot often allow himself. At last, his care found him, and drove him home full of a sharper fear than he had yet felt since the first days. But Mr. Gerald was tranquilly smoking under a palm in the hotel garden, and met him with an easy smile. "She woke once, and said she had had such a pleasant dream. Now she's off again. Do you think we'd better wake her for dinner? I suppose she's getting up her strength in this way. Her sleeping so much is a good symptom, isn't it?"

Lanfear smiled forlornly; neither of them, in view of the possible eventualities, could have said what result they wished the symptoms to favor. But he said: "Decidedly I wouldn't wake her"; and he spent a night of restless sleep penetrated by a nervous expectation which the morning, when it came, rather mockingly defeated.

Miss Gerald appeared promptly at breakfast in their pavilion, with a fresher and gayer look than usual, and to her father's "Well, Nannie, you *have* had a nap, this time," she answered, smiling:

"Have I? It isn't afternoon, is it?"

"No, it's morning. You've napped it all night."

She said: "I can't tell whether I've been asleep or not, sometimes; but now I know I have been; and I feel so rested. Where are we going to-day?"

She turned to Lanfear while her father answered: "I guess the doctor won't want to go very far, to-day, after his expedition yesterday afternoon."

"Ah," she said, "I *knew* you had been somewhere! Was it very far? Are you too tired?"

"It was rather far, but I'm not tired. I shouldn't advise Possana, though."

"Possana?" she repeated. "What is Possana?"

He told her, and then at a jealous look in her eyes he added an account of his excursion. He heightened, if anything, its difficulties, in making light of them as no difficulties for him, and at the end she said, gently: "Shall we go this morning?"

"Let the doctor rest this morning, Nannie," her father interrupted, whimsically, but with what Lanfear knew to be an inner yielding to her will. "Or if you won't let *him*, let *me*. I don't want to go anywhere this morning."

Lanfear thought that he did not wish her to go at all, and hoped that by the afternoon she would have forgotten Possana. She sighed, but in her sigh there was no concession. Then, with the chance of a returning drowse to save him from openly thwarting her will, he merely suggested: "There's plenty of time in the afternoon; the days are so long now; and we can get the sunset from the hills."

"Yes, that will be nice," she said, but he perceived that she did not assent willingly; and there was an effect of resolution in the readiness with which she appeared dressed for the expedition after luncheon. She clearly did not know where they were going, but when she turned to Lanfear with her look of entreaty, he had not the heart to join her father in any conspiracy against her. He beckoned the carriage which had become conscious in its eager driver from the moment she showed herself at the hotel door, and they set out.

When they had left the higher level of the hotel and began their clatter through the long street of the town, Lanfear noted that she seemed to feel as much as himself the quaintness of the little city, rising on one hand, with its narrow alleys under successive arches between the high, dark houses, to the hills, and dropping on the other to sea from the commonplace of the principal thoroughfare, with its pink and white and saffron hotels and shops. Beyond the town their course lay under villa walls, covered with vines and topped by pavilions, and opening finally along a stretch of the old Cornice road.

"But this," she said, at a certain point, "is where we were yesterday!"

"This is where the doctor was yesterday," her father said, behind his cigar.

"And wasn't I with you?" she asked Lanfear.

He said, playfully: "To-day you are. I mustn't be selfish and have you every day."

"Ah, you are laughing at me; but I know I was here yesterday."

Her father set his lips in patience, and Lanfear did not insist.

William Dean Howells

They had halted at this point because, across a wide valley on the shoulder of an approaching height, the ruined village of Possana showed, and lower down and nearer the seat the new town which its people had built when they escaped from the destruction of their world-old home.

World-old it all was, with reference to the human life of it; but the spring-time was immortally young in the landscape. Over the expanses of green and brown fields, and hovering about the gray and white cottages, was a mist of peach and cherry blossoms. Above these the hoar olives thickened, and the vines climbed from terrace to terrace. The valley narrowed inland, and ceased in the embrace of the hills drawing mysteriously together in the distances.

"I think we've got the best part of it here, Miss Gerald," Lanfear broke the common silence by saying. "You couldn't see much more of Possana after you got there."

"Besides," her father ventured a pleasantry which jarred on the younger man, "if you were there with the doctor yesterday, you won't want to make the climb again to-day. Give it up, Nannie!"

"Oh no," she said, "I can't give it up."

"Well, then, we must go on, I suppose. Where do we begin our climb?"

Lanfear explained that he had been obliged to leave his carriage at the foot of the hill, and climb to Possana Nuova by the donkey-paths of the peasants. He had then walked to the ruins of Possana Vecchia, but he suggested that they might find donkeys to carry them on from the new town.

"Well, I hope so," Mr. Gerald grumbled. But at Possana Nuova no saddle-donkeys were to be had, and he announced, at the cafe where they stopped for the negotiation, that he would wait for the young people to go on to Possana Vecchia, and tell him about it when they got back. In the meantime he would watch the game of ball, which, in the piazza before the cafe, appeared to have engaged the energies of the male population. Lanfear was still inwardly demurring, when a stalwart peasant girl came in and announced that she had one donkey which they could have with her own services driving it. She had no saddle, but there was a pad on which the young lady could ride.

"Oh, well, take it for Nannie," Mr. Gerald directed; "only don't be gone too long."

They set out with Miss Gerald reclining in the kind of litter which the donkey proved to be equipped with. Lanfear went beside her, the peasant girl came behind, and at times ran forward to instruct them in the points they seemed to be looking at. For the most part the landscape opened beneath them, but in the azure distances it climbed into Alpine heights which the recent snows had now left to the gloom of their pines. On the slopes of the nearer hills little towns clung, here and there; closer yet farm-houses showed themselves among the vines and olives.

It was very simple, as the life in it must always have been; and Lanfear wondered if the elemental charm of the scene made itself felt by his companion as they climbed the angles of the inclines, in a silence broken only by the picking of the donkey's hoofs on the rude mosaic of the pavement, and the panting of the peasant girl at its heels. On the top of the last upward stretch they stopped for the view, and Miss Gerald asked abruptly: "Why were you so sad?"

"When was I sad?" he asked, in turn.

"I don't know. Weren't you sad?"

"When I was here yesterday, you mean?" She smiled on his fortunate guess, and he said: "Oh, I don't know. It might have begun with thinking—

'Of old, unhappy, far-off things,
And battles long ago.'

You know the pirates used to come sailing over the peaceful sea yonder from Africa, to harry these coasts, and carry off as many as they could capture into slavery in Tunis and Algiers. It was a long, dumb kind of misery that scarcely made an echo in history, but it haunted my fancy yesterday, and I saw these valleys full of the flight and the pursuit which used to fill them, up to the walls of the villages, perched on the heights where men could have built only for safety. Then, I got to thinking of other things—"

"And thinking of things in the past always makes you sad," she said, in pensive reflection. "If it were not for the wearying of always trying to remember, I don't believe I should want my memory back. And of course to be like other people," she ended with a sigh.

It was on his tongue to say that he would not have her so; but he checked himself, and said, lamely enough: "Perhaps you will be like them, sometime."

She startled him by answering irrelevantly: "You know my mother is dead. She died a long while ago; I suppose I must have been very little."

She spoke as if the fact scarcely concerned her, and Lanfear drew a breath of relief in his surprise. He asked, at another tangent: "What made you think I was sad yesterday?"

"Oh, I knew, somehow. I think that I always know when you are sad; I can't tell you how, but I feel it."

"Then I must cheer up," Lanfear said. "If I could only see you strong and well, Miss Gerald, like this girl—"

They both looked at the peasant, and she laughed in sympathy with their smiling, and beat the donkey a little for pleasure; it did not mind.

"But you will be—you will be! We must hurry on, now, or your father will be getting anxious."

They pushed forward on the road, which was now level and wider than it had been. As they drew near the town, whose ruin began more and more to reveal itself in the roofless walls and windowless casements, they saw a man coming towards them, at whose approach Lanfear instinctively put himself forward. The man did not look at them, but passed, frowning darkly, and muttering and gesticulating.

Miss Gerald turned in her litter and followed him with a long gaze. The peasant girl said gayly in Italian: "He is mad; the earthquake made him mad," and urged the donkey forward.

Lanfear, in the interest of science, habitually forbade himself the luxury of anything like foreboding, but now, with the passing of the madman, he felt distinctively a lift from his spirit. He no longer experienced the vague dread which had followed him towards Possana, and made him glad of any delay that kept them from it.

They entered the crooked, narrow street leading abruptly from the open country without any suburban hesitation into the heart of the ruin, which kept a vivid image of uninterrupted mediaeval life. There, till within the actual generation, people had dwelt, winter and summer, as they had dwelt from the beginning of Christian times, with nothing to intimate a domestic or civic advance. This street must have been the main thoroughfare, for stone-paved lanes, still narrower, wound from it here and there, while it kept a fairly direct course to the little piazza on a height in the midst of the town. Two churches and a simple town house partly enclosed it with their seamed and shattered facades. The dwellings here were more ruinous than on the thoroughfare, and some were tumbled in heaps. But Lanfear pushed open the door of one of the churches, and found himself in an interior which, except that it was roofless, could not have been greatly changed since the people had flocked into it to pray for safety from the earthquake. The high altar stood unshaken; around the frieze a succession of stucco cherubs perched, under the open sky, in celestial security.

He had learned to look for the unexpected in Miss Gerald, and he could not have said that it was with surprise he now found her as capable of the emotions which the place inspired, as himself. He made sure of saying: "The earthquake, you know," and she responded with compassion:

"Oh yes; and perhaps that poor man was here, praying with the rest, when it happened. How strange it must all have seemed to them, here where they lived so safely always! They thought such a dreadful thing could happen to others, but not to them. That is the way!"

It seemed to Lanfear once more that she was on the verge of the knowledge so long kept from her. But she went confidently on like a sleepwalker who saves himself from dangers that would be death to him in waking. She spoke of the earthquake as if she had been reading or hearing of it; but he doubted if, with her broken memory, this could be so. It was rather as if she was exploring his own mind in the way of which he had more than once been sensible, and making use of his memory. From time to time she spoke of remembering, but he knew that this was as the blind speak of seeing.

He was anxious to get away, and at last they came out to where they had left the peasant girl waiting beside her donkey. She was not there, and after trying this way and that in the tangle of alleys, Lanfear decided to take the thoroughfare which they had come up by and trust to the chance of finding her at its foot. But he failed even of his search for the street: he came out again and again at the point he had started from.

"What is the matter?" she asked at the annoyance he could not keep out of his face.

He laughed. "Oh, merely that we're lost. But we will wait here till that girl chooses to come back for us. Only it's getting late, and Mr. Gerald—"

"Why, I know the way down," she said, and started quickly in a direction which, as they kept it, he recognized as the route by which he had emerged from the town the day before. He had once more the sense of his memory being used by her, as if being blind, she had taken his hand for guidance, or as if being herself disabled from writing, she had directed a pen in his grasp to form the words she desired to put down. In some mystical sort the effect was hers, but the means was his.

They found the girl waiting with the donkey by the roadside beyond the last house. She explained that, not being able to follow them into the church with her donkey, she had decided to come where they found her and wait for them there.

"Does no one at all live here?" Lanfear asked, carelessly.

"Among the owls and the spectres? I would not pass a night here for a lemonade! My mother," she went on, with a natural pride in the event, "was lost in the earthquake. They found her with me before her breast, and her arms stretched out keeping the stones away." She vividly dramatized the fact. "I was alive, but she was dead."

"Tell her," Miss Gerald said, "that my mother is dead, too."

"Ah, poor little thing!" the girl said, when the message was delivered, and she put her beast in motion, chattering gayly to Miss Gerald in the bond of their common orphanhood.

The return was down-hill, and they went back in half the time it had taken them to come. But even with this speed they were late, and the twilight was deepening when the last turn of their road brought them in sight of the new village. There a wild noise of cries for help burst upon the air, mixed with the shrill sound of maniac gibbering. They saw a boy running towards

William Dean Howells

the town, and nearer them a man struggling with another, whom he had caught about the middle, and was dragging towards the side of the road where it dropped, hundreds of feet, into the gorge below.

The donkey-girl called out: "Oh, the madman! He is killing the signor!"

Lanfear shouted. The madman flung Gerald to the ground, and fled shrieking. Miss Gerald had leaped from her seat, and followed Lanfear as he ran forward to the prostrate form. She did not look at it, but within a few paces she clutched her hands in her hair, and screamed out: "Oh, my mother is killed!" and sank, as if sinking down into the earth, in a swoon.

"No, no; it's all right, Nannie! Look after her, Lanfear! I'm not hurt. I let myself go in that fellow's hands, and I fell softly. It was a good thing he didn't drop me over the edge." Gerald gathered himself up nimbly enough, and lent Lanfear his help with the girl. The situation explained itself, almost without his incoherent additions, to the effect that he had become anxious, and had started out with the boy for a guide, to meet them, and had met the lunatic, who suddenly attacked him. While he talked, Lanfear was feeling the girl's pulse, and now and then putting his ear to her heart. With a glance at her father: "You're bleeding, Mr. Gerald," he said.

"So I am," the old man answered, smiling, as he wiped a red stream from his face with his handkerchief. "But I am not hurt—"

"Better let me tie it up," Lanfear said, taking the handkerchief from him. He felt the unselfish quality in a man whom he had not always thought heroic, and he bound the gash above his forehead with a reverence mingling with his professional gentleness. The donkey-girl had not ceased to cry out and bless herself, but suddenly, as her care was needed in getting Miss Gerald back to the litter, she became a part of the silence in which the procession made its way slowly into Possana Nuova,

Lanfear going on one side, and Mr. Gerald on the other to support his daughter in her place. There was a sort of muted outcry of the whole population awaiting them at the door of the locanda where they had halted before, and which now had the distinction of offering them shelter in a room especially devoted to the poor young lady, who still remained in her swoon.

When the landlord could prevail with his fellow-townsmen and townswomen to disperse in her interest, and had imposed silence upon his customers indoors, Lanfear began his vigil beside his patient in as great quiet as he could anywhere have had. Once during the evening the public physician of the district looked in, but he agreed with Lanfear that nothing was to be done which he was not doing in his greater experience of the case. From time to time Gerald had suggested sending for some San Remo physician in consultation. Lanfear had always approved, and then Gerald had not persisted. He was strongly excited, and anxious not so much for his daughter's recovery from her swoon, which he did not doubt, as for the effect upon her when she should have come to herself.

It was this which he wished to discuss, sitting fallen back into his chair, or walking up and down the room, with his head bound with a bloody handkerchief, and looking, with a sort of alien picturesqueness, like a kindly brigand.

Lanfear did not leave his place beside the bed where the girl lay, white and still as if dead. An inexpressible compassion for the poor man filled his heart. Whatever the event should be, it would be tragical for him. "Go to sleep, Mr. Gerald," he said. "Your waking can do no good. I will keep watch, and if need be, I'll call you. Try to make yourself easy on that couch."

"I shall not sleep," the old man answered. "How could I?" Nevertheless, he adjusted himself to the hard pillows of the lounge where he had been sitting and drowsed among them. He woke just before dawn with a start. "I thought she had come to, and knew everything! What a nightmare! Did I groan? Is there any change?"

Lanfear, sitting by the bed, in the light of the wasting candle, which threw a grotesque shadow of him on the wall, shook his head. After a moment he asked: "How long did you tell me her swoon had lasted after the accident to her mother?"

"I don't think she recovered consciousness for two days, and then she remembered nothing. What do you think are the chances of her remembering now?"

"I don't know. But there's a kind of psychopathic logic—If she lost her memory through one great shock, she might find it through another."

"Yes, yes!" the father said, rising and walking to and fro, in his anguish. "That was what I thought—what I was afraid of. If I could die myself, and save her from living through it—I don't know what I'm saying! But if—but if—if she could somehow be kept from it a little longer! But she can't, she can't! She must know it now when she wakes."

Lanfear had put up his hand, and taken the girl's slim wrist quietly between his thumb and finger, holding it so while her father talked on.

"I suppose it's been a sort of weakness—a sort of wickedness—in me to wish to keep it from her; but I *have* wished that, doctor; you must have seen it, and I can't deny it. We ought to bear what is sent us in this world, and if we escape we must pay for our escape. It has cost her half her being, I know it; but it hasn't cost her her reason, and I'm afraid for that, if she comes into her memory now. Still, you must do—But no one can do anything either to hinder or to help!"

He was talking in a husky undertone, and brokenly, incoherently. He made an appeal, which Lanfear seemed not to hear, where he remained immovable with his hand on the girl's pulse.

"Do you think I am to blame for wishing her never to know it, though without it she must remain deprived of one whole side of life? Do you think my wishing that can have had anything to do with keeping her—But this faint *may* pass and she may wake from it just as she has been. It is logical that she should remember; but is it certain that she will?"

A murmur, so very faint as to be almost no sound at all, came like a response from the girl's lips, and she all but imperceptibly stirred. Her father neither heard nor saw, but Lanfear started forward. He made a sudden clutch at the girl's wrist with the hand that had not left it and then remained motionless. "She will never remember now—here."

He fell on his knees beside the bed and began to sob. "Oh, my dearest! My poor girl! My love!" still keeping her wrist in his hand, and laying his head tenderly on her arm. Suddenly he started, with a shout: "The pulse!" and fell forward, crushing his ear against her heart, and listened with bursts of: "It's beating! She isn't dead! She's alive!" Then he lifted her in his arms, and it was in his embrace that she opened her eyes, and while she clung to him, entreated:

"My father! Where is he?"

A dread fell upon both the men, blighting the joy with which they welcomed her back to life. She took her father's head between her hands, and kissed his bruised face. "I thought you were dead; and I thought that mamma—" She stopped, and they waited breathless. "But that was long ago, wasn't it?"

"Yes," her father eagerly assented. "Very long ago."

"I remember," she sighed. "I thought that I was killed, too. Was it *all* a dream?" Her father and Lanfear looked at each other. Which should speak? "This is Doctor Lanfear, isn't it?" she asked, with a dim smile. "And I'm not dreaming now, am I?" He had released her from his arms, but she held his hand fast. "I know it is you, and papa; and yes, I remember everything. That terrible pain of forgetting is gone! It's beautiful! But did he hurt you badly, papa? I saw him, and I wanted to call to you. But mamma—"

However the change from the oblivion of the past had been operated, it had been mercifully wrought. As far as Lanfear could note it, in the rapture of the new revelation to her which it scarcely needed words to establish, the process was a gradual return from actual facts to the things of yesterday and then to the things of the day before, and so back to the tragedy in which she had been stricken. There was no sudden burst of remembrance, but a slow unveiling of the reality in which her spirit was mystically fortified against it. At times it seemed to him that the effect was accomplished in her by supernatural agencies such as, he remembered once somewhere reading, attend the souls of those lately dead, and explore their minds till every thought and deed of their earthly lives, from the last to the first, is revealed to them out of an inner memory which can never, any jot or tittle, perish. It was as if this had remained in her intact from the blow that shattered her outer remembrance. When the final, long-dreaded horror was reached, it was already a sorrow of the past, suffered and accepted with the resignation which is the close of grief, as of every other passion.

Love had come to her help in the time of her need, but not love alone helped her live back to the hour of that supreme experience and beyond it. In the absorbing interest of her own renascence, the shock, more than the injury which her father had undergone, was ignored, if not neglected. Lanfear had not, indeed, neglected it; but he could not help ignoring it in his happiness, as he remembered afterwards in the self-reproach which he would not let the girl share with him. Nothing, he realized, could have availed if everything had been done which he did not do; but it remained a pang with him that he had so dimly felt his duty to the gentle old man, even while he did it. Gerald lived to witness his daughter's perfect recovery of the self so long lost to her; he lived, with a joy more explicit than their own, to see her the wife of the man to whom she was dearer than love alone could have made her. He lived beyond that time, rejoicing, if it may be so said, in the fond memories of her mother which he had been so long forbidden by her affliction to recall. Then, after the spring of the Riviera had whitened into summer, and San Remo hid, as well as it could, its sunny glare behind its pines and palms, Gerald suffered one long afternoon through the heat till the breathless evening, and went early to bed. He had been full of plans for spending the rest of the summer at the little place in New England where his daughter knew that her mother lay. In the morning he did not wake.

"He gave his life that I might have mine!" she lamented in the first wild grief.

"No, don't say that, Nannie," her husband protested, calling her by the pet name which her father always used. "He is dead; but if we owe each other to his loss, it is because he was given, not because he gave himself."

"Oh, I know, I know!" she wailed. "But he would gladly have given himself for me."

That, perhaps, Lanfear could not have denied, and he had no wish to do so. He had a prescience of happiness for her which the future did not belie; and he divined that a woman must not be forbidden the extremes within which she means to rest her soul.

## II

## THE EIDOLONS OF BROOKS ALFORD

I should like to give the story of Alford's experiences just as Wanhope told it, sitting with us before the glowing hearth in the Turkish room, one night after the other diners at our club had gone away to digest their dinners at the theatre, or in their bachelor apartments up-town, or on the late trains which they were taking north, south, and west; or had hurried back to their offices to spend the time stolen from rest in overwork for which their famished nerves would duly revenge themselves. It was undoubtedly overwork which preceded Alford's experiences if it did not cause them, for he was pretty well broken from it when he took himself off in the early summer, to put the pieces together as best he could by the seaside. But this was a fact which Wanhope was not obliged to note to us, and there were certain other commonplaces of our knowledge of Alford which he could omit without omitting anything essential to our understanding of the facts which he dealt with so delicately, so electly, almost affectionately, coaxing each point into the fittest light, and then lifting his phrase from it, and letting it stand alone in our consciousness. I remember particularly how he touched upon the love-affair which was supposed to have so much to do with Alford's break-up, and how he dismissed it to its proper place in the story. As he talked on, with scarcely an interruption either from the eager credulity of Rulledge or the doubt of Minver, I heard with a sensuous comfort—I can use no other word—the far-off click of the dishes in the club kitchen, putting away till next day, with the musical murmur of a smitten glass or the jingle of a dropped spoon. But if I should try to render his words, I should spoil their impression in the vain attempt, and I feel that it is best to give the story as best I can in words of my own, so far from responsive to the requisitions of the occult incident.

The first intimation Alford had of the strange effect, which from first to last was rather an obsession than a possession of his, was after a morning of idle satisfaction spent in watching the target practice from the fort in the neighborhood of the little fishing-village where he was spending the summer. The target was two or three miles out in the open water beyond the harbor, and he found his pleasure in watching the smoke of the gun for that discrete interval before the report reached him, and then for that somewhat longer interval before he saw the magnificent splash of the shot which, as it plunged into the sea, sent a fan-shaped fountain thirty or forty feet into the air. He did not know and he did not care whether the target was ever hit or not. That fact was no part of his concern. His affair was to watch the burst of smoke from the fort and then to watch the upward gush of water, almost as light and vaporous to the eye, where the ball struck. He did not miss one of the shots fired during the forenoon, and when he met the other people who sat down with him at the midday dinner in the hotel, his talk with them was naturally of the morning's practice. They one and all declared it a great nuisance, and said that it had shattered their nerves terribly, which was not perhaps so strange, since they were all women. But when they asked him in his quality of nervous wreck whether he had not suffered from the prolonged and repeated explosions, too, he found himself able to say no, that he had enjoyed every moment of the firing. He added that he did not believe he had even noticed the noise after the first shot, he was so wholly taken with the beauty of the fountain-burst from the sea which followed; and as he spoke the fan-like spray rose and expanded itself before his eyes, quite blotting out the visage of a young widow across the table. In his swift recognition of the fact and his reflection upon it, he realized that the effect was quite as if he had been looking at some intense light, almost as if he had been looking at the sun, and that the illusion which had blotted out the agreeable reality opposite was of the quality of those flying shapes which repeat themselves here, there, and everywhere that one looks, after lifting the gaze from a dazzling object. When his consciousness had duly registered this perception, there instantly followed a recognition of the fact that the eidolon now filling his vision was not the effect of the dazzled eyes, but of a mental process, of thinking how the thing which it reported had looked.

By the time Alford had co-ordinated this reflection with the other, the eidolon had faded from the lady's face, which again presented itself in uninterrupted loveliness with the added attraction of a distinct pout.

"Well, Mr. Alford!" she bantered him.

"Oh, I beg your pardon! I was thinking—"

"Not of what I was saying," she broke in, laughingly, forgivingly.

"No, I certainly wasn't," he assented, with such a sense of approaching creepiness in his experience that when she challenged him to say what he *was* thinking of, he could not, or would not; she professed to believe that he would not.

In the joking that followed he soon lost the sense of approaching creepiness, and began to be proud of what had happened to him as out of the ordinary, as a species of psychological ecstasy almost of spiritual value. From time to time he tried, by thinking of the splash and upward gush from the cannon-shot's plunge in the sea, to recall the vision, but it would not come again, and at the end of an afternoon somewhat distraughtly spent he decided to put the matter away, as one of the odd things of no significance which happen in life and must be dealt with as mysteries none the less trifling because they are inexplicable.

"Well, you've got over it?" the widow joked him as he drew up towards her, smiling from her rocker on the veranda after supper. At first, all the women in the hotel had petted him; but with their own cares and ailments to reclaim them they let the invalid fall to the peculiar charge of the childless widow who had nothing else to do, and was so well and strong that she could look after the invalid Professor of Archaeology (at the Champlain University) without the fatigues they must feel.

"Yes, I've got over it," he said.

"And what was it?" she boldly pursued.

He was about to say, and then he could not.

"You won't tell?"

"Not yet," he answered. He added, after a moment, "I don't believe I can."

"Because it's confidential?"

"No; not exactly that. Because it's impossible."

"Oh, that's simple enough. I understand exactly what you mean. Well, if ever it becomes less difficult, remember that I should always like to know. It seemed a little—personal."

"How in the world?"

"Well, when one is stared at in that way—"

"Did I stare?"

"Don't you *always* stare? But in this case you stared as if there was something wrong with my hair."

"There wasn't," Alford protested, simple-heartedly. Then he recollected his sophistication to say: "Unless its being of that

William Dean Howells

particular shade between brown and red was wrong."

"Oh, thank you, Mr. Alford! After that I *must* believe you."

They talked on the veranda till the night fell, and then they came in among the lamps, in the parlor, and she sat down with a certain provisionality, putting herself sideways on a light chair by a window, and as she chatted and laughed with one cheek towards him she now and then beat the back of her chair with her open hand. The other people were reading or severely playing cards, and they, too, kept their tones down to a respectful level, while she lingered, and when she rose and said good-night he went out and took some turns on the veranda before going up to bed. She was certainly, he realized, a very pretty woman, and very graceful and very amusing, and though she probably knew all about it, she was the franker and honester for her knowledge.

He had arrived at this conclusion just as he turned the switch of the electric light inside his door, and in the first flash of the carbon film he saw her sitting beside the window in such a chair as she had taken and in the very pose which she had kept in the parlor. Her half-averted face was lit as from laughing, and she had her hand lifted as if to beat the back of her chair.

"Good Heavens, Mrs. Yarrow!" he said, in a sort of whispered shout, while he mechanically closed the door behind him as if to keep the fact to himself. "What in the world are you doing here?"

Then she was not there. Nothing was there; not even a chair beside the window.

Alford dropped weakly into the only chair in the room, which stood next the door by the head of his bed, and abandoned himself a helpless prey to the logic of the events.

It was at this point, which I have been able to give in Wanhope's exact words, that, in the ensuing pause, Rulledge asked, as if he thought some detail might be denied him: "And what was the logic of the events?"

Minver gave a fleering laugh. "Don't be premature, Rulledge. If you have the logic now, you will spoil everything. You can't have the moral until you've had the whole story. Go on, Wanhope. You're so much more interesting than usual that I won't ask how you got hold of all these compromising minutiae."

"Of course," Wanhope returned, "they're not for the general ear. I go rather further, for the sake of the curious fact, than I should be warranted in doing if I did not know my audience so well."

We joined in a murmur of gratification, and he went on to say that Alford's first coherent thought was that he was dreaming one of those unwarranted dreams in which we make our acquaintance privy to all sorts of strange incidents. Then he knew that he was not dreaming, and that his eye had merely externated a mental vision, as in the case of the cannon-shot splash of which he had seen the phantom as soon as it was mentioned. He remembered afterwards asking himself in a sort of terror how far it was going to go with him; how far his thought was going to report itself objectively hereafter, and what were the reasonable implications of his abnormal experiences. He did not know just how long he sat by his bedside trying to think, only to have his conclusions whir away like a flock of startled birds when he approached them. He went to bed because he was exhausted rather than because he was sleepy, but he could not recall a moment of wakefulness after his head touched the pillow.

He woke surprisingly refreshed, but at the belated breakfast where he found Mrs. Yarrow still lingering he thought her looking not well. She confessed, listlessly, that she had not rested well. She was not sure, she said, whether the sea air agreed with her; she might try the mountains a little later. She was not inclined to talk, and that day he scarcely spoke with

William Dean Howells

her except in commonplaces at the table. They had no return to the little mystery they had mocked together the day before.

More days passed, and Alford had no recurrence of his visions. His acquaintance with Mrs. Yarrow made no further advance; there was no one else in the hotel who interested him, and he bored himself. At the same time his recovery seemed retarded; he lost tone, and after a fortnight he ran up to talk himself over with his doctor in Boston. He rather thought he would mention his eidolons, and ask if they were at all related to the condition of his nerves. It was a keen disappointment, but it ought not to have been a surprise, for him to find that his doctor was off on his summer vacation. The caretaker who opened the door to Alford named a young physician in the same block of Marlborough Street who had his doctor's practice for the summer, but Alford had not the heart to go to this alternate.

He started down to his hotel on a late afternoon train that would bring him to the station after dusk, and before he reached it the lamps had been lighted in his car. Alford sat in a sparsely peopled smoker, where he had found a place away from the crowd in the other coaches, and looked out of the window into the reflected interior of his car, which now and then thinned away and let him see the weeds and gravel of the railroad banks, with the bushes that topped them and the woods that backed them. The train at one point stopped rather suddenly and then went on, for no reason that he ever cared to inquire; but as it slowly moved forward again he was reminded of something he had seen one night in going to New York just before the train drew into Springfield. It had then made such another apparently reasonless stop; but before it resumed its course Alford saw from his window a group of trainmen, and his own Pullman conductor with his lantern on his arm, bending over the figure of a man defined in his dark clothing against the snow of the bank where he lay propped. His face was waxen white, and Alford noted how particularly black the mustache looked traversing the pallid visage. He never knew whether the man was killed or merely stunned; you learn nothing with certainty of such things on trains; but now, as he thought of the incident, its eidolon showed itself outside of his mind, and followed him in every detail, even to a snowy stretch of the embankment, until the increasing speed of the train seemed to sweep it back out of sight.

Alford turned his eyes to the interior of the smoker, which, except for two or three dozing commuters and a noisy euchre-party, had been empty of everything but the fumes and stale odors of tobacco, and found it swarming with visions, the eidolons of everything he remembered from his past life. Whatever had once strongly impressed itself upon his nerves was reported there again as instantly as he thought of it. It was largely a whirling chaos, a kaleidoscopic jumble of facts; but from time to time some more memorable and important experience visualized itself alone. Such was the death-bed of the little sister whom he had been wakened, a child, to see going to heaven, as they told him. Such was the pathetic, foolish face of the girl whom long ago he had made believe he cared for, and then had abruptly broken with: he saw again, with heartache, her silly, tender amaze when he said he was going away. Such was the look of mute astonishment, of gentle reproach, in the eyes of the friend, now long dead, whom in a moment of insensate fury he had struck on the mouth, and who put his hand to his bleeding lips as he bent that gaze of wonder and bewilderment upon him. But it was not alone the dreadful impressions that reported themselves. There were others, as vivid, which came back in the original joyousness: the face of his mother looking up at him from the crowd on a day of college triumph when he was delivering the valedictory of his class; the collective gayety of the whole table on a particularly delightful evening at his dining-club; his own image in the glass as he caught sight of it on coming home accepted by the woman who afterwards jilted him; the transport which lighted up his father's visage when he stepped ashore from the vessel which had been rumored lost, and he could be verified by the senses as still alive; the comical, bashful ecstasy of the good fellow, his ancient chum, in telling him he had had a son born the night before, and the mother

William Dean Howells

was doing well, and how he laughed and danced, and skipped into the air.

The smoker was full of these eidolons and of others which came and went with constant vicissitude. But what was of a greater weirdness than seeing them within it was seeing them without in that reflection of the interior which travelled with it through the summer night, and repeated it, now dimly, now brilliantly, in every detail. Alford sat in a daze, with a smile which he was aware of, fixed and stiff as if in plaster, on his face, and with his gaze bent on this or that eidolon, and then on all of them together. He was not so much afraid of them as of being noticed by the other passengers in the smoker, to whom he knew he might look very queer. He said to himself that he was making the whole thing, but the very subjectivity was what filled him with a deep and hopeless dread. At last the train ceased its long leaping through the dark, and with its coming to a stand the whole illusion vanished. He heard a gay voice which he knew bidding some one good-bye who was getting into the car just back of the smoker, and as he descended to the platform he almost walked into the arms of Mrs. Yarrow.

"Why, Mr. Alford! We had given you up. We thought you wouldn't come back till to-morrow—or perhaps ever. What in the world will you do for supper? The kitchen fires were out ages ago!"

In the light of the station electrics she beamed upon him, and he felt glad at heart, as if he had been saved from something, a mortal danger or a threatened shame. But he could not speak at once; his teeth closed with tetanic force upon each other. Later, as they walked to the hotel, through the warm, soft night in which the south wind was roaming the starless heavens for rain, he found his voice, and although he felt that he was speaking unnaturally, he made out to answer the lively questions with which she pelted him too thickly to expect them to be answered severally. She told him all the news of the day, and when she began on yesterday's news she checked herself with a laugh and said she had forgotten that he had only been gone since morning. "But now," she said, "you see how you've been missed—how *any* man must be missed in a hotel full of women."

She took charge of him when they got to the house, and said if he would go boldly into the dining-room, where they detected, as they approached, one lamp scantly shining from the else darkened windows, she would beard the lioness in her den, by which she meant the cook in the kitchen, and see what she could get him for supper. Apparently she could get nothing warm, for when a reluctant waitress appeared it was with such a chilly refection on her tray that Alford, though he was not very hungry, returned from interrogating the obscurity for eidolons, and shivered at it. At the same time the swing-door of the long, dim room opened to admit a gush of the outer radiance on which Mrs. Yarrow drifted in with a chafing-dish in one hand and a tea-basket in the other. She floated tiltingly towards him like, he thought, a pretty little ship, and sent a cheery hail before.

"I've been trying to get somebody to join you at a premature Welsh-rarebit and a belated cup of tea, but I can't tear one of the tabbies from their cards or the kittens from their gambols in the amusement-hall in the basement. Do you mind so very much having it alone? Because you'll have to, whether you do or not. Unless you call me company, when I'm merely cook."

She put her utensils on the table beside the forbidding tray the waitress had left, and helped lift herself by pressing one hand on the top of a chair towards the electric, which she flashed up to keep the dismal lamp in countenance. Alford let her do it. He durst not, he felt, stir from his place, lest any movement should summon back the eidolons; and now in the sudden glare of light he shyly, slyly searched the room for them. Not one, fair or foul, showed itself, and slowly he felt a great weight lifting from his heart. In its place there sprang up a joyous gratitude towards Mrs. Yarrow, who had saved him from them, from himself. An inexpressible tenderness filled his breast; the tears rose to his eyes; a soft glow enveloped his whole being, a warmth of hope, a freshness of life renewed, encompassed him. He wished to take her in his arms, to tell her how he loved her; and as she bustled about, lighting the lamp of her chafing-dish, and kindling the little spirit-stove she had brought with her to make tea, he let his gaze dwell upon every pose, every motion of her with a glad hunger in which no smallest detail was lost. He now believed that without her he must die, without her he could not wish to live.

"Jove," Rulledge broke in at this point of Wanhope's story, which I am telling again so badly, "I think Alford was in luck."

Minver gave a harsh cackle. "The only thing Rulledge finds fault with in this club is 'the lack of woman's nursing and the lack of woman's tears.' Nothing is wanting to his enjoyment of his victuals but the fact that they are not served by a neat-handed Phyllis, like Alford's."

Rulledge glanced towards Wanhope, and innocently inquired, "Was that her first name?"

Minver burst into a scream, and Rulledge looked red and silly for having given himself away; but he made an excursion to the buffet outside, and returned with a sandwich with which he supported himself stolidly under Minver's derision, until Wanhope came to his relief by resuming his story, or rather his study, of Alford's strange experience.

Mrs. Yarrow first gave Alford his tea, as being of a prompter brew than the rarebit, but she was very quick and apt with that, too; and pretty soon she leaned forward, and in the glow from the lamp under the chafing-dish, which spiritualized her charming face with its thin radiance, puffed the flame out with her pouted lips, and drew back with a long-sighed "There! That will make you see your grandmother, if anything will."

"My grandmother?" Alford repeated.

"Yes. Wouldn't you like to?" Mrs.. Yarrow asked, pouring the thick composition over the toast (rescued stone-cold from the frigid tray) on Alford's plate. "I'm sure I should like to see mine—dear old gran! Not that I ever saw her—either of her— or should know how she looked. Did you ever see yours— either of her?" she pursued, impulsively.

"Oh yes," Alford answered, looking intently at her, but with so little speculation in the eyes he glared so with that he knew her to be uneasy under them.

She laughed a little, and stayed her hand on the bail of the teapot. "Which of her?"

"Oh, both!"

"And—and—did she look so much like *me*?" she said, with an added laugh, that he perceived had an hysterical note in it. "You're letting your rarebit get cold!"

He laughed himself, now, a great laugh of relaxation, of relief. "Not the least in the world! She was not exactly a phantom of delight."

"Oh, thank you, Mr. Alford. Now, it's your tea's getting cold."

They laughed together, and he gave himself to his victual with a relish that she visibly enjoyed. When that question of his grandmother had been pushed he thought of an awful experience of his childhood, which left on his infant mind an indelible impression, a scar, to remain from the original wound forever. He had been caught in a lie, the first he could remember, but by no means the last, by many immemorable thousands. His poor little wickedness had impugned the veracity of both these terrible old ladies, who, habitually at odds with each other, now united, for once, against him. He could always see himself, a mean little blubbering-faced rascal, stealing guilty looks of imploring at their faces, set unmercifully against him, one in sorrow and one in anger, requiring his mother to whip him, and insisting till he was led, loudly roaring, into the parlor, and there made a liar of for all time, so far as fear could do it.

When Mrs. Yarrow asked if he had ever seen his grandmother he expected instantly to see her, in duplicate, and as a sole refuge, but with little hope that it would save him, he kept his eyes fast on hers, and to his unspeakable joy it did avail. No other face, of sorrow or of anger, rose between them. For the time his thought was quit of its consequence; no eidolon outwardly repeated his inward vision. A warm gush of gratitude seemed to burst from his heart, and to bathe his whole being, and then to flow in a tide of ineffable tenderness towards Mrs. Yarrow, and involve her and bear them together heavenward. It was not passion, it was not love, he perceived well enough; it was the utterance of a vital conviction that she had saved him from an overwhelming subjective horror, and that in her sweet objectivity there was a security and peace to be found nowhere else.

He greedily ate every atom of his rarebit, he absorbed every drop of the moisture in the teapot, so that when she shook it and shook it, and then tried to pour something from it, there was no slightest dribble at the spout. But they lingered, talking and laughing, and perhaps they might never have left the place if the hard handmaiden who had brought the tea-tray had not first tried putting her head in at the swing-door from the kitchen, and then, later, come boldly in and taken the tray away.

Mrs. Yarrow waited self-respectfully for her disappearance, and then she said, "I'm afraid that was a hint, Mr. Alford."

"It seemed like one," he owned.

They went out together, gayly chatting, but she would not encourage the movement he made towards the veranda. She remained firmly attached to the newel-post of the stairs, and at the first chance he gave her she said good-night and bounded lightly upward. At the turn of the stairs she stopped and looked laughing down at him over the rail. "I hope you won't see your grandmother."

"Oh, not a bit of it," he called back. He felt that he failed to give his reply the quality of epigram, but he was not unhappy in his failure.

Many light-hearted days followed this joyous evening. No eidolons haunted Alford's horizon, perhaps because Mrs. Yarrow filled his whole heaven. She was very constantly with him, guiding his wavering steps up the hill of recovery, which he climbed with more and more activity, and keeping him company in those valleys of relapse into which he now and then fell back from the difficult steeps. It came to be tacitly, or at least passively, conceded by the other ladies that she had somehow earned the exclusive right to what had once been the common charge; or that if one of their number had a claim to keep Mr. Alford from killing himself by all sorts of imprudences, which in his case amounted to impieties, it was certainly Mrs. Yarrow. They did not put this in terms, but they felt it and acted it.

She was all the safer guardian for a delicate invalid because she loathed manly sports so entirely that she did not even pretend to like them, as most women, poor things, think themselves obliged to do. In her hands there was no danger that he would be tempted to excesses in golf. She was really afraid of all boats, but she was willing to go out with him in the sail-boat of a superannuated skipper, because to sit talking in the stern and stoop for the vagaries of the boom in tacking was such good exercise. She would join him in fishing from the rotting pier, but with no certainty which was a cunner and which was a sculpin, when she caught it, and with an equal horror of both the nasty, wriggling things. When they went a walk together, her notion of a healthful tramp was to find a nice place among the sweet-fern or the pine-needles, and sit down in it and talk, or make a lap, to which he could bring the berries he gathered for her to arrange in the shallow leaf-trays she pinned together with twigs. She really preferred a rocking-chair on the veranda to anything else; but if he wished to go to those other excesses, she would go with him, to keep him out of mischief.

There could be only one credible reading of the situation, but Alford let the summer pass in this pleasant dreaming without waking up till too late to the pleasanter reality. It will seem strange enough, but it is true, that it was no part of his dream to fancy that Mrs. Yarrow was in love with him. He knew very well, long before the end, that he was in love with her; but, remaining in the dark otherwise, he considered only himself in forbearing verbally to make love to her.

"Well!" Rulledge snarled at this point, "he *was* a chump."

Wanhope at the moment opposed nothing directly to the censure, but said that something pathetically reproachful in Mrs. Yarrow's smiling looks penetrated to Alford as she nodded gayly from the car window to him in the little group which had assembled to see her off at the station when she left, by no means the first of their happy hotel circle to go.

"Somebody," Rulledge burst out again, "ought to have kicked him."

"What's become," Minver asked, "of all the dear maids and widows that you've failed to marry at the end of each summer, Rulledge?"

The satire involved flattery so sweet that Rulledge could not perhaps wish to make any retort. He frowned sternly, and said, with a face averted from Minver: "Go on, Wanhope!"

Wanhope here permitted himself a philosophical excursion in which I will not accompany him. It was apparently to prepare us for the dramatic fact which followed, and which I suppose he was trying rather to work away from than work up to. It included some facts which he had failed to touch on before, and which led to a discussion very interesting in itself, but of a range too great for the limits I am trying to keep here. It seems that Alford had been stayed from declaring his love not only because he doubted of its nature, but also because he questioned whether a man in his broken health had any right to offer himself to a woman, and because from a yet finer scruple he hesitated in his poverty to ask the hand of a rich woman. On the first point, we were pretty well agreed, but on the second we divided again, especially Rulledge and Minver, who held, the one, that his hesitation did Alford honor, and quite relieved him from the imputation of being a chump; and the other that he was an ass to keep quiet for any such silly reason. Minver contended that every woman had a right, whether rich or poor, to the man who loved her; and, moreover, there were now so many rich women that, if they were not allowed to marry poor men, their chances of marriage were indefinitely reduced. What better could a widow do with the money she had inherited from a husband she probably did not love than give it to a man like Alford—or to an ass like Alford, Minver corrected himself.

His *reductio ad absurdum* allowed Wanhope to resume with a laugh, and say that Alford waited at the station in the singleness to which the tactful dispersion of the others had left him, and watched the train rapidly dwindle in the perspective, till an abrupt turn of the road carried it out of sight. Then he lifted his eyes with a long sigh, and looked round. Everywhere he saw Mrs. Yarrow's smiling face with that inner pathos. It swarmed upon him from all points; and wherever he turned it repeated itself in the distances like that succession of faces you see when you stand between two mirrors.

It was not merely a lapse from his lately hopeful state with Alford, it was a collapse. The man withered and dwindled away, till he felt that he must audibly rattle in his clothes as he walked by people. He did not walk much. Mostly he remained shrunken in the arm-chair where he used to sit beside Mrs. Yarrow's rocker, and the ladies, the older and the older-fashioned, who were "sticking it out" at the hotel till it should close on the 15th of September, observed him, some

William Dean Howells

compassionately, some censoriously, but all in the same conviction.

"It's plain to be seen what ails Mr. Alford, *now*."

"Well, I guess it *is*."

"*I* guess so."

"I *guess* it is."

"Seems kind of heartless, her going and leaving him so."

"Like a sick kitten!"

"Well, I should say as *much*."

"Your eyes bother you, Mr. Alford?" one of them chanted, breaking from their discussion of him to appeal directly to him. He was rubbing his eyes, to relieve himself for the moment from the intolerable affliction of those swarming eidolons, which, whenever he thought of this thing or that, thickened about him. They now no longer displaced one another, but those which came first remained fadedly beside or behind the fresher appearances, like the earlier rainbow which loses depth and color when a later arch defines itself.

"Yes," he said, glad of the subterfuge. "They annoy me a good deal of late."

"You want to get fitted for a good pair of glasses. I kept letting it go, when I first began to get old-sighted."

Another lady came to Alford's rescue. "I guess Mr. Alford has no need to get fitted for old sight yet a while. You got little spidery things—specks and dots—in your eyes?"

"Yes—multitudes," he said, hopelessly.

"Well, I'll tell you what: you want to build up. That was the way with me, and the oculist said it was from getting all run down. I built up, and the first thing I knew my sight was as clear as a bell. You want to build up."

"You want to go to the mountains," a third interposed. "That's where Mrs. Yarrow's gone, and I guess it'll do her more good than sticking it out here would ever have done."

Alford would have been glad enough to go to the mountains, but with those illusions hovering closer and closer about him, he had no longer the courage, the strength. He had barely enough of either to get away to Boston. He found his doctor this time, after winning and losing the wager he made himself that he would not have returned to town yet, and the good-fortune was almost too much for his shaken nerves. The cordial of his friend's greeting—they had been chums at Harvard—completed his overthrow. As he sank upon the professional sofa, where so many other cases had been diagnosticated, he broke into tears. "Hello, old fellow!" the doctor said, encouragingly, and more tenderly than he would have dealt with some women. "What's up?"

"Jim," Alford found voice to say, "I'm afraid I'm losing my mind."

The doctor smiled provisionally. "Well, that's *one* of the signs you're not. Can you say how?"

"Oh yes. In a minute," Alford sobbed, and when he had got the better of himself he told his friend the whole story. In the direct examination he suppressed Mrs. Yarrow's part, but when the doctor, who had listened with smiling seriousness, began to cross-examine him with the question, "And you don't remember that any outside influence affected the recurrence of the illusions, or did anything to prevent it?" Alford answered promptly: "Oh yes. There was a woman who did."

"A woman? What sort of a woman?"

William Dean Howells

Alford told.

"That is very curious," the doctor said. "I know a man who used to have a distressing dream. He broke it up by telling his wife about it every morning after he had dreamt it."

"Unluckily, she isn't my wife," Alford said, gloomily.

"But when she was with you, you got rid of the illusions?"

"At first, I used to see hers; then I stopped seeing any."

"Did you ever tell her of them?"

"No; I didn't."

"Never tell anybody?"

"No one but you."

"And do you see them now?"

"No."

"Do you think, because you've told me of them?"

"It seems so."

The doctor was silent for a marked space. Then he asked, smiling: "Well, why not?"

"Why not what?"

"Tell your wife."

"How, my wife?"

"By marriage."

Alford looked dazed. "Do you mean Mrs. Yarrow?"

"If that's her name, and she's a widow."

"And do you think it would be the fair thing for a man on the verge of insanity—a physical and mental wreck—to ask a woman to marry him?"

"In your case, yes. In the first place, you're not so bad as all that. You need nothing but rest for your body and change for your mind. I believe you'll get rid of your illusions as soon as you form the habit of speaking of them promptly when they begin to trouble you. You ought to speak of them to some one. You can't always have me around, and Mrs. Yarrow would be the next best thing."

"She's rich, and you know what I am. I'll have to borrow the money to rest on, I'm so poor."

"Not if you marry it."

Alford rose, somewhat more vigorously than he had sat down. But that day he did not go beyond ascertaining that Mrs. Yarrow was in town. He found out the fact from the maid at her door, who said that she was nearly always at home after dinner, and, without waiting for the evening of another day, Alford went to call upon her.

She said, coming down to him in a rather old-fashioned, impersonal drawing-room which looked distinctly as if it had been left to her: "I was so glad to get your card. When did you leave Woodbeach?"

"Mrs. Yarrow," he returned, as if that were the answer, "I think I owe you an explanation."

"Pay it!" she bantered, putting out her hand.

"I'm so poverty-stricken that I don't know whether I can. Did you ever notice anything odd about me?"

His directness seemed to have a right to directness from her. "I noticed that you stared a good deal—or used to. But people *do* stare."

"I stared because I saw things."

"Saw things?"

"I saw whatever I thought of. Whatever came into my mind was externated in a vision."

She smiled, he could not make out whether uneasily or not. "It sounds rather creepy, doesn't it? But it's very interesting."

"That's what the doctor said; I've been to see him this morning. May I tell you about my visions? They're not so creepy as they sound, I believe, and I don't think they'll keep you awake."

"Yes, do," she said. "I should like of all things to hear about them. Perhaps I've been one of them."

"You have."

"Oh! Isn't that rather personal?"

"I hope not offensively."

He went on to tell her, with even greater fulness than he had told the doctor. She listened with the interest women take in anything weird, and with a compassion for him which she did not conceal so perfectly but that he saw it. At the end he said: "You may wonder that I come to you with all this, which must sound like the ravings of a madman."

"No—no," she hesitated.

"I came because I wished you to know everything about me before—before—I wouldn't have come, you'll believe me, if I hadn't had the doctor's assurance that my trouble was merely a part of my being physically out of kilter, and had nothing to do with my sanity—Good Heavens! What am I saying? But the thought has tormented me so! And in the midst of it I've allowed myself to—Mrs. Yarrow, I love you. Don't you know that?"

Alford may have had a divided mind in this declaration, but after that one word Mrs. Yarrow had no mind for anything else. He went on.

"I'm not only sick—so sick that I sha'n't be able to do any work for a year at least—but I'm poor, so poor that I can't afford to be sick."

She lifted her eyes and looked at him, where she sat oddly aloof from those possessions of hers, to which she seemed so little related, and said, with a smile quivering at the corners of her pretty mouth, "I don't see what that has to do with it."

"What do you mean?" He stared at her hard.

"Am I in duplicate or triplicate, this time?"

"No, you're only one, and there's none like you! I could never see any one else while I looked at you!" he cried, only half aware of his poetry, and meaning what he said very literally.

But she took only the poetry. "I shouldn't wish you to," she said, and she laughed.

He could not believe yet in his good-fortune. His countenance fell. "I'm afraid I don't understand, or that you don't. It doesn't seem as if I could get to the end of my unworthiness, which isn't voluntary. It seems altogether too base. I can't let you say what you do, if you mean it, till you know that I come to you in despair as well as in love. You saved me from the fear

William Dean Howells

I was in, again and again, and I believe that without you I shall—Ah, it seems very base! But the doctor—If I could always tell some one—if I could tell *you* when these things were obsessing me—haunting me—they would cease—"

Mrs. Yarrow rose, with rather a piteous smile. "Then, I am a prescription!" She hoped, woman-like, that she was solely a passion; but is any woman worth having, ever solely a passion?

"Don't!" Alford implored, rising too. "Don't, in mercy, take it that way! It's only that I wish you to know everything that's in me; to know how utterly helpless and worthless I am. You needn't have a pang in throwing such a thing away."

She put out her hand to him, but at arm's-length. "I sha'n't throw you away—at least, not to-night. I want to think." It was a way of saying she wished him to go, and he had no desire to stay. He asked if he might come again, and she said, "Oh yes."

"To-morrow?"

"Not to-morrow, perhaps. When I send. Was it *young* Doctor Enderby?"

They had rather a sad, dry parting; and when her door closed upon him he felt that it had shut him out forever. His shame and his defeat were so great that he did not think of his eidolons, and they did not come to trouble him. He woke in the morning, asking himself, bitterly, if he were cured already. His humiliation was such that he closed his eyes to the light, and wished he might never again open them to it.

The question that Mrs. Yarrow had to ask Dr. Enderby was not the question he had instantly forecast for her when she put aside her veil in his office and told him who she was. She did not seem anxious to be assured of Alford's mental condition, or as to any risks in marrying him. Her inquiry was much more psychological; it was almost impersonal, and yet Dr.

Enderby thought she looked as if she had been crying.

She had a difficulty in formulating her question, and when it came it was almost a speculation.

"Women," she said, a little hoarsely, "have no right, I suppose, to expect the ideal in life. The best they can do seems to be to make the real look like it."

Dr. Enderby reflected. "Well, yes. But I don't know that I ever put it to myself in just those terms."

Then she remarked, as if that were the next thing: "You've known Mr. Alford a long time."

"We were at school together, and we shared the same rooms in Harvard."

"He is very sincere," she added, as if this were relevant.

"He's a man who likes to have a little worse than the worst known about him. One might say he was excessively sincere." Enderby divined that Alford had been bungling the matter, and he was willing to help him out if he could.

Mrs. Yarrow fixed dimly beautiful eyes upon him. "I don't know," she said, "why it wouldn't be ideal—as much ideal as anything—to give one's self absolutely to—to—a duty—or not duty, exactly; I don't mean that. Especially," she added, showing a light through the mist, "if one wanted to do it."

Then he knew she had made up her mind, and though on some accounts he would have liked to laugh with her, on other accounts he felt that he owed it to her to be serious.

"If women could not fulfil the ideal in that way—if they did not constantly do it—there would be no marriages for love."

"Do you think so?" she asked, with a shaking voice. "But

men—men are ideal, too."

"Not as women are—except now and then some fool like Alford." Now, indeed, he laughed, and he began to praise Alford from his heart, so delicately, so tenderly, so reverently, that Mrs. Yarrow laughed too before he was done, and cried a little, and when she rose to leave she could not speak; but clung to his hand, on turning away, and so flung it from behind her with a gesture that Enderby thought pretty.

At this point, Wanhope stopped as if that were the end.

"And did she let Alford come to see her again?" Rulledge, at once romantic and literal, demanded.

"Oh yes. At any rate, they were married that fall. They are—I believe he's pursuing his archaeological studies there—living in Athens."

"Together?" Minver smoothly inquired.

At this expression of cynicism Rulledge gave him a look that would have incinerated another. Wanhope went out with Minver, and then, after a moment's daze, Rulledge exclaimed: "Jove! I forgot to ask him whether it's stopped Alford's illusions!"

# III

## A MEMORY THAT WORKED OVERTIME

Minver's brother took down from the top of the low bookshelf a small painting on panel, which he first studied in the obverse, and then turned and contemplated on the back with the same dreamy smile. "I don't see how that got *here*," he said, absently.

"Well," Minver returned, "you don't expect *me* to tell you, except on the principle that any one would naturally know more about anything of yours than you would." He took it from his brother and looked at the front of it. "It isn't bad. It's pretty good!" He turned it round. "Why, it's one of old Blakey's! How did *you* come by it?"

"Stole it, probably," Minver's brother said, still thoughtfully. Then with an effect of recollecting: "No, come to think of it," he added, "Blakey gave it to me." The Minvers played these little comedies together, quite as much to satisfy their tenderness for each other as to give their friends pleasure. "Think you're the only painter that gets me to take his truck as a gift? He gave it to me, let's see, about ten years ago, when he was trying to make a die of it, and failed; I thought he would succeed. But it's been in my wife's room nearly ever since, and what I can't understand is what she's doing with it down here."

"Probably to make trouble for you, somehow," Minver suggested.

William Dean Howells

"No, I don't think it's *that*, quite," his brother returned, with a false air of scrupulosity, which was part of their game with each other. He looked some more at the picture, and then he glanced from it at me. "There's a very curious story connected with that sketch."

"Oh, well, tell it," Minver said. "Tell it! I suppose I can stand it again. Acton's never heard it, I believe. But you needn't make a show of sparing him. I *couldn't* stand that."

"I certainly haven't heard the story," I said, "and if I had I would be too polite to own it."

Minver's brother looked towards the open door over his shoulder, and Minver interpreted for him: "She's not coming. I'll give you due warning."

"It was before we were married, but not much before, and the picture was a sort of wedding present for my wife, though Blakey made a show of giving it to me. Said he had painted it for me, because he had a prophetic soul, and felt in his bones that I was going to want a picture of the place where I first met her. You see, it's the little villa her mother had taken that winter on the Viale Petrarca, just outside of Florence. It *was* the first place I met her, but not the last."

"Don't be obvious," Minver ordered.

His brother did not mind him. "I thought it was mighty nice of Blakey. He was barking away, all the time he was talking, and when he wasn't coughing he was so hoarse he could hardly speak above a whisper; but he kept talking on, and wishing me happy, and fending off my gratitude, while he was finding a piece of manila paper to wrap the sketch in, and then hunting for a piece of string to tie it. When he handed it to me at last, he gasped out: 'I don't mind her knowing that I partly meant it as the place where *she* first met *you*, too. I'm not ashamed of it as a bit of color. Anyway, I sha'n't live to do anything better.'"

"'Oh, yes, you will,' I came back in that lying way we think is kind with dying people. I suppose it is; anyway, it turned out all right with Blakey, as he'll testify if you look him up when you go to Florence. By the way, he lives in that villa *now*."

"No?" I said. "How charming!"

Minver's brother went on: "I made up my mind to be awfully careful of that picture, and not let it out of my hand till I left it with 'her' mother, to be put among the other wedding presents that were accumulating at their house in Exeter Street. So I held it on my lap going in by train from Lexington, where Blakey lived, and when I got out at the old Lowell Depot— North Station, now—and got into the little tinkle-tankle horse-car that took me up to where I was to get the Back Bay car—Those were the prehistoric times before trolleys, and there were odds in horse-cars. We considered the blue-painted Back Bay cars very swell. *You* remember them?" he asked Minver.

"Not when I can help it," Minver answered. "When I broke with Boston, and went to New York, I burnt my horse-cars behind me, and never wanted to know what they looked like, one from another."

"Well, as I was saying," Minver's brother went on, without regarding his impatriotism, "when I got into the horse-car at the depot, I rushed for a corner seat, and I put the picture, with its face next the car-end, between me and the wall, and kept my hand on it; and when I changed to the Back Bay car, I did the same thing. There was a florist's just there, and I couldn't resist some Mayflowers in the window; I was in that condition, you know, when flowers seemed to be made for her, and I had to take her own to her wherever I found them. I put the bunch between my knees, and kept one hand on it, while I kept my other hand on the picture at my side. I was feeling first-rate, and when General Filbert got in after we started, and stood before me hanging by a strap and talking down to me, I had the decency to propose giving him my seat, as he was about ten years older."

"Sure?" Minver asked.

"Well, say fifteen. I don't pretend to be a chicken, and never did. But he wouldn't hear of it. Said I had a bundle, and winked at the bunch of Mayflowers. We had such a jolly talk that I let the car carry me a block by and had to get out at Gloucester and run back to Exeter. I rang, and, when the maid came to the door, there I stood with nothing but the Mayflowers in my hand."

"Good *coup de theatre*," Minver jeered. "Curtain?"

His brother disdained reply, or was too much absorbed in his tale to think of any. "When the girl opened the door and I discovered my fix I burst out, 'Good Lord!' and I stuck the bunch of flowers at her, and turned and ran. I suppose I must have had some notion of overtaking the car with my picture in it. But the best I could do was to let the next one overtake me several blocks down Marlborough Street, and carry me to the little jumping-off station on Westchester Park, as we used to call it in those days, at the end of the Back Bay line.

"As I pushed into the railroad office, I bet myself that the picture would not be there, and, sure enough, I won."

"You were always a lucky dog," Minver said.

"But the man in charge was very encouraging, and said it was sure to be turned in; and he asked me what time the car had passed the corner of Gloucester Street. I happened to know, and then he said, Oh yes, that conductor was a substitute, and he wouldn't be on again till morning; then he would be certain to bring the picture with him. I was not to worry, for it would be all right. Nothing left in the Back Bay cars was ever lost; the character of the abutters was guarantee for that, and they were practically the only passengers. The conductors and the drivers were as honest as the passengers, and I could consider myself in the hands of friends."

"He was so reassuring that I went away smiling at my fears, and promising to be round bright and early, as soon, the official suggested—the morrow being Sunday—as soon as the men and horses had had their baked beans."

"Still, after dinner, I had a lurking anxiety, which I turned into a friendly impulse to go and call on Mrs. Filbert, whom I really owed a bread-and-butter visit, and who, I knew, would not mind my coming in the evening. The general, she said, had been telling her of our pleasant chat in the car, and would be glad to smoke his after-dinner cigar with me, and why wouldn't I come into the library?"

"We were so very jolly together, all three, that I made light of my misadventure about the picture. The general inquired about the flowers first. He remembered the flowers perfectly, and hoped they were acceptable; he thought he remembered the picture, too, now I mentioned it; but he would not have noticed it so much, there by my side, with my hand on it. I would be sure to get it. He gave several instances, personal to him and his friends, of recoveries of lost articles; it was really astonishing how careful the horse-car people were, especially on the Back Bay line. I would find my picture all right at the Westchester Park station in the morning; never fear."

"I feared so little that I slept well, and even overslept; and I went to get my picture quite confidently, and I could hardly believe it had not been turned in yet, though the station-master told me so. The substitute conductor had not seen it, but more than likely it was at the stables, where the cleaners would have found it in the car and turned it in. He was as robustly cheerful about it as ever, and offered to send an inquiry by the next car; but I said, Why shouldn't I go myself; and he said that was a good idea. So I went, and it was well I did, for my picture was not there, and I had saved time by going. It was not there, but the head man said I need not worry a mite about it; I was certain to get it sooner or later; it

William Dean Howells

would be turned in, to a dead certainty. We became rather confidential, and I went so far as to explain about wanting to make my inquiries very quietly on Blakey's account: he would be annoyed if he heard of its loss, and it might react unfavorably on his health."

"The head man said that was so; and he would tell me what I wanted to do: I wanted to go to the Company's General Offices in Milk Street, and tell them about it. That was where everything went as a last resort, and he would bet any money that I would see my picture there the first thing I got inside the door. I thanked him with the fervor I thought he merited, and said I would go at once."

"'Well,' he said, 'you don't want to go to-day, you know. The offices are not open Sunday. And to-morrow's a holiday. But you're all right. You'll find your picture there, don't you have any doubts about it.'"

"That was my next to last Sunday supper with my wife, before she became my wife, at her mother's house, and I went to the feast with as little gayety as I suppose any young man ever carried to a supper of the kind. I was told, afterwards, that my behavior up to a certain point was so suggestive either of secret crime or of secret regret, that the only question was whether they should have in the police or I should be given back my engagement ring and advised to go. Luckily I ceased to bear my anguish just in time."

"The fact is, I could not stand it any longer, and as soon as I was alone with her I made a clean breast of it; partially clean, that is: I suppose a fellow never tells *all* to a girl, if he truly loves her." Minver's brother glanced round at us and gathered the harvest of our approving smiles. "I said to her, 'I've been having a wedding present.' 'Well,' she said, 'you've come as near having no use for a wedding present as anybody *I* know. Was having a wedding present what made you so gloomy at supper? Who gave it to you, anyway?' 'Old Blakey.' 'A painting?' 'Yes—a sketch.' 'What of?' This was where I qualified. I said: 'Oh, just one of those Sorrento things of his.' You see, if I told her that it was the villa where we first met, and then said I had left it in the horse-car, she would take it as proof positive that I did not really care anything about her or I never could have forgotten it."

"You were wise as far as you went," Minver said. "Go on."

"Well, I told her the whole story circumstantially: how I had kept the sketch religiously in my lap in the train, and then held it down with my hand all the while beside me in the first horse-car, and did the same thing in the Back Bay car I changed to; and felt of it the whole time I was talking with General Filbert, and then left it there when I got out to leave the flowers at her door, when the awful fact came over me like a flash. 'Yes,' she said, 'Norah said you poked the flowers at her without a word, and she had to guess they were for me.'"

"I had got my story pretty glib by this time; I had reeled it off with increasing particulars to the Westchester Park station-master, and the head man at the stables, and General Filbert, and I was so letter-perfect that I had a vision of the whole thing, especially of my talking with the general while I kept my hand on the picture—and then all was dark."

"At the end she said we must advertise for the picture. I said it would kill Blakey if he saw it; and she said: No matter, *let* it kill him; it would show him that we valued his gift, and were moving heaven and earth to find it; and, at any rate, it would kill *me* if I kept myself in suspense. I said I should not care for that; but with her sympathy I guessed I could live through the night, and I was sure I should find the thing at the Milk Street office in the morning."

"'Why,' said she, 'to-morrow it'll be shut!' and then I didn't really know what to say, and I agreed to drawing up an advertisement then and there, so as not to lose an instant's time after I had been at the Milk Street office on Tuesday and found the picture had not been turned in. She said I could

William Dean Howells

dictate the advertisement and she would write it down, and she asked: 'Which one of his Sorrento things was it? You must describe it exactly, you know.' That made me feel awfully, and I said I was not going to have my next-to-last Sunday evening with her spoiled by writing advertisements; and I got away, somehow, with all sorts of comforting reassurances from her. I could see that she was feigning them to encourage me."

"The next morning, I simply could not keep away from the Milk Street office, and my unreasonable impatience was rewarded by finding it at least ajar, if not open. There was the nicest kind of a young fellow there, and he said he was not officially present; but what could he do for me? Then I told him the whole story, with details I had not thought of before; and he was just as enthusiastic about my getting my picture as the Westchester Park station-master or the head man of the stables. It was morally certain to be turned in, the first thing in the morning; but he would take a description of it, and send out inquiries to all the conductors and drivers and car-cleaners, and make a special thing of it. He entered into the spirit of the affair, and I felt that I had such a friend in him that I confided a little more and hinted at the double interest I had in the picture. I didn't pretend that it was one of Blakey's Sorrento things, but I gave him a full and true description of it, with its length, breadth, and thickness, in exact measure."

Here Minver's brother stopped and lost himself in contemplation of the sketch, as he held it at arm's-length.

"Well, did you get your picture?" I prompted, after a moment.

"Oh yes," he said, with a quick turn towards me. "This is it. A District Messenger brought it round the first thing Tuesday morning. He brought it," Minver's brother added, with a certain effectiveness, "from the florist's, where I had stopped to get those Mayflowers. I had left it there."

"You've told it very well, this time, Joe," Minver said. "But Acton here is waiting for the psychology. Poor old Wanhope ought to be here," he added to me. He looked about for a match to light his pipe, and his brother jerked his head in the direction of the chimney.

"Box on the mantel. Yes," he sighed, "that was really something very curious. You see, I had invented the whole history of the case from the time I got into the Back Bay car with my flowers. Absolutely nothing had happened of all I had remembered till I got out of the car. I did not put the picture beside me at the end of the car; I did not keep my hand on it while I talked with General Filbert; I did not leave it behind me when I left the car. Nothing of the kind happened. I had already left it at the florist's, and that whole passage of experience which was so vividly and circumstantially stamped in my memory that I related it four or five times over, and would have made oath to every detail of it, was pure invention, or, rather, it was something less positive: the reflex of the first half of my horse-car experience, when I really did put the picture in the corner next me, and did keep my hand on it."

"Very strange," I was beginning, but just then the door opened and Mrs. Minver came in, and I was presented.

She gave me a distracted hand, as she said to her husband: "Have you been telling the story about that picture again?" He was still holding it. "Silly!"

She was a mighty pretty woman, but full of vim and fun and sense.

"It's one of the most curious freaks of memory I ever heard of, Mrs. Minver," I said.

Then she showed that she was proud of it, though she had called him silly. "Have you told," she demanded of her husband, "how oddly your memory behaved about the subject of the picture, too?"

"I have again eaten that particular piece of humble-pie,"

William Dean Howells

Minver's brother replied.

"Well," she said to me, "*I* think he was simply so possessed with the awfulness of having lost the picture that all the rest took place prophetically, but unconsciously."

"By a species of inverted presentiment?" I suggested.

"Yes," she assented, slowly, as if the formulation were new to her, but not unacceptable. "Something of that kind. I never heard of anybody else having it."

Minver had got his pipe alight, and was enjoying it. "*I* think Joe was simply off his nut, for the time being."

# IV

## A CASE OF METAPHANTASMIA

The stranger was a guest of Halson's, and Halson himself was a comparative stranger, for he was of recent election to our dining-club, and was better known to Minver than to the rest of our little group, though one could not be sure that he was very well known to Minver. The stranger had been dining with Halson, and we had found the two smoking together, with their cups of black coffee at their elbows, before the smouldering fire in the Turkish room when we came in from dinner—my friend Wanhope the psychologist, Rulledge the sentimentalist, Minver the painter, and myself. It struck me for the first time that a fire on the hearth was out of keeping with a Turkish room, but I felt that the cups of black coffee restored the lost balance in some measure.

Before we had settled into our wonted places—in fact, almost as we entered—Halson looked over his shoulder and said: "Mr. Wanhope, I want you to hear this story of my friend's. Go on, Newton—or, rather, go back and begin again—and I'll introduce you afterwards."

The stranger made a becoming show of deprecation. He said he did not think the story would bear immediate repetition, or was even worth telling once, but, if we had nothing better to do, perhaps we might do worse than hear it; the most he could say for it was that the thing really happened. He wore a large, drooping, gray mustache, which, with the imperial below it, quite hid his mouth, and gave him, somehow, a martial effect, besides accurately dating him of the period between the latest sixties and earliest seventies, when his beard would have been black; I liked his mustache not being stubbed in the modern manner, but allowed to fall heavily over his lips, and then branch away from the corners of his mouth as far as it would. He lighted the cigar which Halson gave him, and, blowing the bitten-off tip towards the fire, began:

"It was about that time when we first had a ten-o'clock night train from Boston to New York." Train used to start at nine, and lag along round by Springfield, and get into the old Twenty-sixth Street Station here at six in the morning, where they let you sleep as long as you liked. They call you up now at half-past five, and, if you don't turn out, they haul you back to Mott Haven, or New Haven, I'm not sure which. I used to go into Boston and turn in at the old Worcester Depot, as we called it then, just about the time the train began to move, and I usually got a fine night's rest in the course of the nine or ten hours we were on the way to New York; it didn't seem quite the same after we began saying Albany Depot: shortened up the run, somehow.

"But that night I wasn't very sleepy, and the porter had got the place so piping hot with the big stoves, one at each end of the car, to keep the good, old-fashioned Christmas cold out, that I thought I should be more comfortable with a smoke before I went to bed; and, anyhow, I could get away from the heat better in the smoking-room. I hated to be leaving home on Christmas Eve, for I never had done that before, and I hated to be leaving my wife alone with the children and the two girls in our little house in Cambridge. Before I started in on the old horse-car for Boston, I had helped her to tuck the young ones in and to fill the stockings hung along the wall over the register—the nearest we could come to a fireplace—and I thought those stockings looked very weird, five of them, dangling lumpily down, and I kept seeing them, and her sitting up sewing in front of them, and afraid to go to bed on account of burglars. I suppose she was shyer of burglars than any woman ever was that had never seen a sign of them. She was always calling me up, to go down-stairs and put them out, and I used to wander all over the house, from attic to cellar, in my nighty, with a lamp in one hand and a poker in the other, so that no burglar could have missed me if he had wanted an easy mark. I always kept a lamp and a poker handy."

The stranger heaved a sigh as of fond reminiscence, and looked round for the sympathy which in our company of bachelors he failed of; even the sympathetic Rulledge failed of the necessary experience to move him in compassionate response.

"Well," the stranger went on, a little damped perhaps by his failure, but supported apparently by the interest of the fact in hand, "I had the smoking-room to myself for a while, and then a fellow put his head in that I thought I knew after I had thought I didn't know him. He dawned on me more and more, and I had to acknowledge to myself, by and by, that it was a man named Melford, whom I used to room with in Holworthy at Harvard; that is, we had an apartment of two bedrooms and a study; and I suppose there were never two fellows knew less of each other than we did at the end of our four years together. I can't say what Melford knew of me, but the most I knew of Melford was his particular brand of nightmare."

Wanhope gave the first sign of his interest in the matter. He took his cigar from his lips, and softly emitted an "Ah!"

Rulledge went further and interrogatively repeated the word "Nightmare?"

"Nightmare," the stranger continued, firmly. "The curious thing about it was that I never exactly knew the subject of his nightmare, and a more curious thing yet was Melford himself never knew it, when I woke him up. He said he couldn't make out anything but a kind of scraping in a door-lock. His theory was that in his childhood it had been a much completer thing, but that the circumstances had broken down in a sort of decadence, and now there was nothing left of it but that scraping in the door-lock, like somebody trying to turn a misfit key. I used to throw things at his door, and once I tried a cold-water douche from the pitcher, when he was very hard to waken; but that was rather brutal, and after a while I used to let him roar himself awake; he would always do it, if I trusted to nature; and before our junior year was out I got so that I could sleep through, pretty calmly; I would just say to myself when he fetched me to the surface with a yell, 'That's Melford dreaming,' and doze off sweetly."

"Jove!" Rulledge said, "I don't see how you could stand it."

"There's everything in habit, Rulledge," Minver put in. "Perhaps our friend only dreamt that he heard a dream."

"That's quite possible," the stranger owned, politely. "But the case is superficially as I state it. However, it was all past, long ago, when I recognized Melford in the smoking-room that night: it must have been ten or a dozen years. I was wearing a full beard then, and so was he; we wore as much beard as we could in those days. I had been through the war since college, and he had been in California, most of the time, and, as he told me, he had been up north, in Alaska, just after we bought it, and hurt his eyes—had snow-blindness—and he wore spectacles. In fact, I had to do most of the recognizing, but after we found out who we were we were rather comfortable; and I liked him better than I remembered to have liked him in our college days. I don't suppose there was ever much harm in him; it was only my grudge about his nightmare. We talked along and smoked along for about an hour, and I could hear the porter outside, making up the berths, and the train rumbled away towards Framingham, and then towards Worcester, and I began to be sleepy, and to think I would go to bed myself; and just then the door of the smoking-room opened, and a young girl put in her face a moment, and said: 'Oh, I beg your pardon. I thought it was the stateroom,' and then she shut the door, and I realized that she looked like a girl I used to know."

The stranger stopped, and I fancied from a note in his voice that this girl was perhaps like an early love. We silently waited for him to resume how and when he would. He sighed, and after an appreciable interval he began again. "It is curious how things are related to one another. My wife had never seen her, and yet, somehow, this girl that looked like the one I mean brought my mind back to my wife with a quick turn, after I had forgotten her in my talk with Melford for the time being. I thought how lonely she was in that little house of ours in Cambridge, on rather an outlying street, and I knew she was thinking of me, and hating to have me away on Christmas Eve, which isn't such a lively time after you're grown up and begin to look back on a good many other Christmas Eves, when you were a child yourself; in fact, I don't know a dismaler night in the whole year. I stepped out on the platform before I began to turn in, for a mouthful of the night air, and I found it was spitting snow—a regular Christmas Eve of the true pattern; and I didn't believe, from the business feel of those hard little pellets, that it was going to stop in a hurry, and I thought if we got into New York on time we should be lucky. The snow made me think of a night when my wife was sure there were burglars in the house; and in fact I heard their tramping on the stairs myself—thump, thump, thump, and then a stop, and then down again. Of course it was the slide and thud of the snow from the roof of the main part of the house to the roof of the kitchen, which was in an L, a story lower, but it was as good an imitation of burglars as I want to hear at one o'clock in the morning; and the recollection of it made me more anxious about my wife, not because I believed she was in danger, but because I knew how frightened she must be.

"When I went back into the car, that girl passed me on the way to her stateroom, and I concluded that she was the only woman on board, and her friends had taken the stateroom for her, so that she needn't feel strange. I usually go to bed in a sleeper as I do in my own house, but that night I somehow couldn't. I got to thinking of accidents, and I thought how disagreeable it would be to turn out into the snow in my nighty. I ended by turning in with my clothes on, all except my coat; and, in spite of the red-hot stoves, I wasn't any too warm. I had a berth in the middle of the car, and just as I was parting my curtains to lie down, old Melford came to take the lower berth opposite. It made me laugh a little, and I was glad of the relief. 'Why, hello, Melford,' said I. 'This is like the old Holworthy times.' 'Yes, isn't it?' said he, and then I asked something that I had kept myself from asking all through our talk in the smoking-room, because I knew he was rather sensitive about it, or used to be. 'Do you ever have that regulation nightmare of yours nowadays, Melford? He gave a laugh, and said: 'I haven't had it, I suppose, once in ten years. What made you think of it?' I said: 'Oh, I don't know. It just came into my mind. Well, good-night, old fellow. I hope you'll rest well,' and suddenly I began to feel light-hearted again, and I went to sleep as gayly as ever I did in my life."

The stranger paused again, and Wanhope said: "Those swift transitions of mood are very interesting. Of course they occur in that remote region of the mind where all incidents and sensations are of one quality, and things of the most opposite character unite in a common origin. No one that I remember has attempted to trace such effects to their causes, and then back again from their causes, which would be much more important."

"Yes, I dare say," Minver put in. "But if they all amount to the same thing in the end, what difference would it make?"

"It would perhaps establish the identity of good and evil," Wanhope suggested.

"Oh, the sinners are convinced of that already," Minver said, while Rulledge glanced quickly from one to the other.

The stranger looked rather dazed, and Rulledge said: "Well, I don't suppose that was the conclusion of the whole matter?"

"Oh no," the stranger answered, "that was only the beginning of the conclusion. I didn't go to sleep at once, though I felt so much at peace. In fact, Melford beat me, and I could hear him far in advance, steaming and whistling away, in a style that I recalled as characteristic, over a space of intervening years that I hadn't definitely summed up yet. It made me think of a night near Narragansett Bay, where two friends of mine and I had had a mighty good dinner at a sort of wild club-house, and had hurried into our bunks, each one so as to get the start of the others, for the fellows that were left behind knew they had no chance of sleep after the first began to get in his work. I laughed, and I suppose I must have gone to sleep almost simultaneously, for I don't recollect anything afterwards till I was wakened by a kind of muffled bellow, that I remembered only too well. It was the unfailing sign of Melford's nightmare."

"I was ready to swear, and I was ashamed for the fellow who had no more self-control than that: when a fellow snores, or has a nightmare, you always think first off that he needn't have had it if he had tried. As usual, I knew Melford didn't know what his nightmare was about, and that made me madder still, to have him bellowing into the air like that, with no particular aim. All at once there came a piercing scream from the stateroom, and then I knew that the girl there had heard Melford and been scared out of a year's growth."

The stranger made a little break, and Wanhope asked, "Could you make out what she screamed, or was it quite inarticulate?"

"It was plain enough, and it gave me a clew, somehow, to what Melford's nightmare was about. She was calling out, 'Help! help! help! Burglars!' till I thought she would raise the roof of the car."

"And did she wake anybody?" Rulledge inquired.

"That was the strange part of it. Not a soul stirred, and after the first burst the girl seemed to quiet down again and yield the floor to Melford, who kept bellowing steadily away. I was so furious that I reached out across the aisle to shake him, but the attempt was too much for me. I lost my balance and fell out of my berth onto the floor. You may imagine the state of mind I was in. I gathered myself up and pulled Melford's curtains open and was just going to fall on him tooth and nail, when I was nearly taken off my feet again by an apparition: well, it looked like an apparition, but it was a tall fellow in his nighty—for it was twenty years before pajamas—and he had a small dark lantern in his hand, such as we used to carry in those days so as to read in our berths when we couldn't sleep. He was gritting his teeth, and growling between them: 'Out o' this! Out o' this! I'm going to shoot to kill, you blasted thieves!' I could see by the strange look in his eyes that he was sleep-walking, and I didn't wait to see if he had a pistol. I popped in behind the curtains, and found myself on top of another fellow, for I had popped into the wrong berth in my confusion. The man started up and yelled: 'Oh, don't kill me! There's my watch on the stand, and all the money in the house is in my pantaloons pocket. The silver's in the sideboard down-stairs, and it's plated, anyway.' Then I understood what his complaint was, and I rolled onto the floor again. By that time every man in the car was out of his berth, too, except Melford, who was devoting himself strictly to business; and every man was grabbing some other, and shouting, 'Police!' or 'Burglars!' or 'Help!' or 'Murder!' just as the fancy took him."

"Most extraordinary!" Wanhope commented as the stranger paused for breath.

In the intensity of our interest, we had crowded close upon him, except Minver, who sat with his head thrown back, and that cynical cast in his eye which always exasperated Rulledge; and Halson, who stood smiling proudly, as if the stranger's story did him as his sponsor credit personally.

"Yes," the stranger owned, "but I don't know that there wasn't something more extraordinary still. From time to time the girl in the stateroom kept piping up, with a shriek for help. She had got past the burglar stage, but she wanted to be saved, anyhow, from some danger which she didn't specify. It went through me that it was very strange nobody called the porter, and I set up a shout of 'Porter!' on my own account. I decided that if there were burglars the porter was the man to put them out, and that if there were no burglars the porter could relieve our groundless fears. Sure enough, he came rushing in, as soon as I called for him, from the little corner by the smoking-room where he was blacking boots between dozes. He was wide enough awake, if having his eyes open meant that, and he had a shoe on one hand and a shoe-brush in the other. But he merely joined in the general up-roar and shouted for the police."

"Excuse me," Wanhope interposed. "I wish to be clear as to the facts. You had reasoned it out that the porter could quiet the tumult?"

"Never reasoned anything out so clearly in my life."

"But what was your theory of the situation? That your friend, Mr. Melford, had a nightmare in which he was dreaming of burglars?"

"I hadn't a doubt of it."

"And that by a species of dream-transference the nightmare was communicated to the young lady in the stateroom?"

"Well—yes."

"And that her call for help and her cry of burglars acted as a sort of hypnotic suggestion with the other sleepers, and they began to be afflicted with the same nightmare?"

"I don't know that I ever put it to myself so distinctly, but it appears to me now that I must have reached some such conclusion."

"That is very interesting, very interesting indeed. I beg your pardon. Please go on," Wanhope courteously entreated.

William Dean Howells

"I don't remember just where I was," the stranger faltered.

Rulledge returned with an accuracy which obliged us all: "The porter merely joined in the general uproar and shouted for the police."

"Oh yes," the stranger assented. "Then I didn't know what to do, for a minute. The porter was a pretty thick-headed darky, but he was lion-hearted; and his idea was to lay hold of a burglar wherever he could find him. There were plenty of burglars in the aisle there, or people that were afraid of burglars, and they seemed to think the porter had a good idea. They had hold of one another already, and now began to pull up and down the aisles in a way that reminded me of the old-fashioned mesmeric lecturers, when they told their subjects that they were this or that, and set them to acting the part. I remembered how once when the mesmerist gave out that they were at a horse—race, and his subjects all got astride of their chairs, and galloped up and down the hall like a lot of little boys on laths. I thought of that now, and although it was rather a serious business, for I didn't know what minute they would come to blows, I couldn't help laughing. The sight was weird enough. Every one looked like a somnambulist as he pulled and hauled. The young lady in the stateroom was doing her full share. She was screaming, 'Won't somebody let me out?' and hammering on the door. I guess it was her screaming and hammering that brought the conductor at last, or maybe he just came round in the course of nature to take up the tickets. It was before the time when they took the tickets at the gate, and you used to stick them into a little slot at the side of your berth, and the conductor came along and took them in the night, somewhere between Worcester and Springfield, I should say."

"I remember," Rulledge assented, but very carefully, so as not to interrupt the flow of the narrative. "Used to wake up everybody in the car."

"Exactly," the stranger said. "But this time they were all wide awake to receive him, or fast asleep, and dreaming their roles. He came along with the wire of his lantern over his arm, the way the old-time conductors did, and calling out, 'Tickets!' just as if it was broad day, and he believed every man was trying to beat his way to New York. The oddest thing about it was that the sleep-walkers all stopped their pulling and hauling a moment, and each man reached down to the little slot alongside of his berth and handed over his ticket. Then they took hold and began pulling and hauling again. I suppose the conductor asked what the matter was; but I couldn't hear him, and I couldn't make out exactly what he did say. But the passengers understood, and they all shouted 'Burglars!' and that girl in the stateroom gave a shriek that you could have heard from one end of the train to the other, and hammered on the door, and wanted to be let out."

"It seemed to take the conductor by surprise, and he faced towards the stateroom and let the lantern slip off his arm, and it dropped onto the floor and went out; I remember thinking what a good thing it didn't set the car on fire. But there in the dark—for the car lamps went out at the same time with the lantern—I could hear those fellows pulling and hauling up and down the aisle and scuffling over the floor, and through all Melford bellowing away, like an orchestral accompaniment to a combat in Wagner opera, but getting quieter and quieter till his bellow died away altogether. At the same time the row in the aisle of the car stopped, and there was perfect silence, and I could hear the snow rattling against my window. Then I went off into a sound sleep, and never woke till we got into New York."

The stranger seemed to have reached the end of his story, or at least to have exhausted the interest it had for him, and he smoked on, holding his knee between his hands and looking thoughtfully into the fire.

He had left us rather breathless, or, better said, blank, and each looked at the other for some initiative; then we united in looking at Wanhope; that is, Rulledge and I did. Minver rose and stretched himself with what I must describe as a sardonic yawn; Halson had stolen away before the end, as one to whom the end was known. Wanhope seemed by no means averse to the inquiry delegated to him, but only to be formulating its terms. At last he said:

"I don't remember hearing of any case of this kind before. Thought-transference is a sufficiently ascertained phenomenon —the insistence of a conscious mind upon a certain fact until it penetrates the unconscious mind of another and is adopted as its own. But in the dream state the mind seems passive, and becomes the prey of this or that self-suggestion, without the power of imparting it to another dreaming mind. Yet here we have positive proof of such an effect. It appears that the victim of a particularly terrific nightmare was able to share its horrors—or rather unable *not* to share them—with a whole sleeping-car full of people whose brains helplessly took up the same theme, and dreamed it, as we may say, to the same conclusions. I said proof, but of course we can't accept a single instance as establishing a scientific certainty. I don't question the veracity of Mr.—"

"Newton," the stranger suggested.

"Newton's experience," Wanhope continued, "but we must wait for a good many cases of the kind before we can accept what I may call metaphantasmia as being equally established with thought-transference. If we could it would throw light upon a whole series of most curious phenomena, as, for instance, the privity of a person dreamed about to the incident created by the dreamer."

"That would be rather dreadful, wouldn't it?" I ventured. "We do dream such scandalous, such compromising things about people."

"All that," Wanhope gently insisted, "could have nothing to do with the fact. That alone is to be considered in an inquiry of the kind. One is never obliged to tell one's dreams. I wonder"—he turned to the stranger, who sat absently staring into the fire—"if you happened to speak to your friend about his nightmare in the morning, and whether he was by any chance aware of the participation of the others in it?"

"I certainly spoke to him pretty plainly when we got into New York."

"And what did he say?"

"He said he had never slept better in his life, and he couldn't remember having a trace of nightmare. He said he heard *me* groaning at one time, but I stopped just as he woke, and so he didn't rouse me as he thought of doing. It was at Hartford, and he went to sleep again, and slept through without a break."

"And what was your conclusion from that?" Wanhope asked.

"That he was lying, I should say," Rulledge replied for the stranger.

Wanhope still waited, and the stranger said, "I suppose one conclusion might be that I had dreamed the whole thing myself."

"Then you wish me to infer," the psychologist pursued, "that the entire incident was a figment of your sleeping brain? That there was no sort of sleeping thought-transference, no metaphantasmia, no—Excuse me. Do you remember verifying your impression of being between Worcester and Springfield when the affair occurred, by looking at your watch, for instance?"

The stranger suddenly pulled out his watch at the word. "Good Heavens!" he called out. "It's twenty minutes of eleven, and I have to take the eleven-o'clock train to Boston. I must bid you good-evening, gentlemen. I've just time to get it if I can catch a cab. Good-night, good-night. I hope if you come to Boston—eh—Good-night! Sometimes," he called over his shoulder, "I've thought it might have been that girl in the stateroom that started the dreaming."

He had wrung our hands one after another, and now he ran out of the room.

Rulledge said, in appeal to Wanhope: "I don't see how his being the dreamer invalidates the case, if his dreams affected the others."

"Well," Wanhope answered, thoughtfully, "that depends."

"And what do you think of its being the girl in the stateroom?"

"That would be very interesting."

# V

## EDITHA

The air was thick with the war feeling, like the electricity of a storm which has not yet burst. Editha sat looking out into the hot spring afternoon, with her lips parted, and panting with the intensity of the question whether she could let him go. She had decided that she could not let him stay, when she saw him at the end of the still leafless avenue, making slowly up towards the house, with his head down and his figure relaxed. She ran impatiently out on the veranda, to the edge of the steps, and imperatively demanded greater haste of him with her will before she called aloud to him: "George!"

He had quickened his pace in mystical response to her mystical urgence, before he could have heard her; now he looked up and answered, "Well?"

"Oh, how united we are!" she exulted, and then she swooped down the steps to him. "What is it?" she cried.

"It's war," he said, and he pulled her up to him and kissed her.

She kissed him back intensely, but irrelevantly, as to their passion, and uttered from deep in her throat. "How glorious!"

"It's war," he repeated, without consenting to her sense of it; and she did not know just what to think at first. She never knew what to think of him; that made his mystery, his charm.

William Dean Howells

All through their courtship, which was contemporaneous with the growth of the war feeling, she had been puzzled by his want of seriousness about it. He seemed to despise it even more than he abhorred it. She could have understood his abhorring any sort of bloodshed; that would have been a survival of his old life when he thought he would be a minister, and before he changed and took up the law. But making light of a cause so high and noble seemed to show a want of earnestness at the core of his being. Not but that she felt herself able to cope with a congenital defect of that sort, and make his love for her save him from himself. Now perhaps the miracle was already wrought in him. In the presence of the tremendous fact that he announced, all triviality seemed to have gone out of him; she began to feel that. He sank down on the top step, and wiped his forehead with his handkerchief, while she poured out upon him her question of the origin and authenticity of his news.

All the while, in her duplex emotioning, she was aware that now at the very beginning she must put a guard upon herself against urging him, by any word or act, to take the part that her whole soul willed him to take, for the completion of her ideal of him. He was very nearly perfect as he was, and he must be allowed to perfect himself. But he was peculiar, and he might very well be reasoned out of his peculiarity. Before her reasoning went her emotioning: her nature pulling upon his nature, her womanhood upon his manhood, without her knowing the means she was using to the end she was willing. She had always supposed that the man who won her would have done something to win her; she did not know what, but something. George Gearson had simply asked her for her love, on the way home from a concert, and she gave her love to him, without, as it were, thinking. But now, it flashed upon her, if he could do something worthy to *have* won her—be a hero, *her* hero—it would be even better than if he had done it before asking her; it would be grander. Besides, she had believed in the war from the beginning.

"But don't you see, dearest," she said, "that it wouldn't have come to this if it hadn't been in the order of Providence? And I call any war glorious that is for the liberation of people who have been struggling for years against the cruelest oppression. Don't you think so, too?"

"I suppose so," he returned, languidly. "But war! Is it glorious to break the peace of the world?"

"That ignoble peace! It was no peace at all, with that crime and shame at our very gates." She was conscious of parroting the current phrases of the newspapers, but it was no time to pick and choose her words. She must sacrifice anything to the high ideal she had for him, and after a good deal of rapid argument she ended with the climax: "But now it doesn't matter about the how or why. Since the war has come, all that is gone. There are no two sides any more. There is nothing now but our country."

He sat with his eyes closed and his head leant back against the veranda, and he remarked, with a vague smile, as if musing aloud, "Our country—right or wrong."

"Yes, right or wrong!" she returned, fervidly. "I'll go and get you some lemonade." She rose rustling, and whisked away; when she came back with two tall glasses of clouded liquid on a tray, and the ice clucking in them, he still sat as she had left him, and she said, as if there had been no interruption: "But there is no question of wrong in this case. I call it a sacred war. A war for liberty and humanity, if ever there was one. And I know you will see it just as I do, yet."

He took half the lemonade at a gulp, and he answered as he set the glass down: "I know you always have the highest ideal. When I differ from you I ought to doubt myself."

A generous sob rose in Editha's throat for the humility of a man, so very nearly perfect, who was willing to put himself below her.

William Dean Howells

Besides, she felt, more subliminally, that he was never so near slipping through her fingers as when he took that meek way.

"You shall not say that! Only, for once I happen to be right." She seized his hand in her two hands, and poured her soul from her eyes into his. "Don't you think so?" she entreated him.

He released his hand and drank the rest of his lemonade, and she added, "Have mine, too," but he shook his head in answering, "I've no business to think so, unless I act so, too."

Her heart stopped a beat before it pulsed on with leaps that she felt in her neck. She had noticed that strange thing in men: they seemed to feel bound to do what they believed, and not think a thing was finished when they said it, as girls did. She knew what was in his mind, but she pretended not, and she said, "Oh, I am not sure," and then faltered.

He went on as if to himself, without apparently heeding her: "There's only one way of proving one's faith in a thing like this."

She could not say that she understood, but she did understand.

He went on again. "If I believed—if I felt as you do about this war—Do you wish me to feel as you do?"

Now she was really not sure; so she said: "George, I don't know what you mean."

He seemed to muse away from her as before.

"There is a sort of fascination in it. I suppose that at the bottom of his heart every man would like at times to have his courage tested, to see how he would act."

"How can you talk in that ghastly way?"

"It *is* rather morbid. Still, that's what it comes to, unless you're swept away by ambition or driven by conviction. I haven't the conviction or the ambition, and the other thing is what it comes to with me. I ought to have been a preacher, after all; then I couldn't have asked it of myself, as I must, now I'm a lawyer. And you believe it's a holy war, Editha?" he suddenly addressed her. "Oh, I know you do! But you wish me to believe so, too?"

She hardly knew whether he was mocking or not, in the ironical way he always had with her plainer mind. But the only thing was to be outspoken with him.

"George, I wish you to believe whatever you think is true, at any and every cost. If I've tried to talk you into anything, I take it all back."

"Oh, I know that, Editha. I know how sincere you are, and how—I wish I had your undoubting spirit! I'll think it over; I'd like to believe as you do. But I don't, now; I don't, indeed. It isn't this war alone; though this seems peculiarly wanton and needless; but it's every war—so stupid; it makes me sick. Why shouldn't this thing have been settled reasonably?"

"Because," she said, very throatily again, "God meant it to be war."

"You think it was God? Yes, I suppose that is what people will say."

"Do you suppose it would have been war if God hadn't meant it?"

"I don't know. Sometimes it seems as if God had put this world into men's keeping to work it as they pleased."

"Now, George, that is blasphemy."

"Well, I won't blaspheme. I'll try to believe in your pocket

William Dean Howells

Providence," he said, and then he rose to go.

"Why don't you stay to dinner?" Dinner at Balcom's Works was at one o'clock.

"I'll come back to supper, if you'll let me. Perhaps I shall bring you a convert."

"Well, you may come back, on that condition."

"All right. If I don't come, you'll understand."

He went away without kissing her, and she felt it a suspension of their engagement. It all interested her intensely; she was undergoing a tremendous experience, and she was being equal to it. While she stood looking after him, her mother came out through one of the long windows onto the veranda, with a catlike softness and vagueness.

"Why didn't he stay to dinner?"

"Because—because—war has been declared," Editha pronounced, without turning.

Her mother said, "Oh, my!" and then said nothing more until she had sat down in one of the large Shaker chairs and rocked herself for some time. Then she closed whatever tacit passage of thought there had been in her mind with the spoken words: "Well, I hope *he* won't go."

"And *I* hope he *will*," the girl said, and confronted her mother with a stormy exaltation that would have frightened any creature less unimpressionable than a cat.

Her mother rocked herself again for an interval of cogitation. What she arrived at in speech was: "Well, I guess you've done a wicked thing, Editha Balcom."

The girl said, as she passed indoors through the same window her mother had come out by: "I haven't done anything—yet."

*　*　*　*　*

In her room, she put together all her letters and gifts from Gearson, down to the withered petals of the first flower he had offered, with that timidity of his veiled in that irony of his. In the heart of the packet she enshrined her engagement ring which she had restored to the pretty box he had brought it her in. Then she sat down, if not calmly yet strongly, and wrote:

> "GEORGE:—I understood when you left me. But I think we had better emphasize your meaning that if we cannot be one in everything we had better be one in nothing. So I am sending these things for your keeping till you have made up your mind.

> "I shall always love you, and therefore I shall never marry any one else. But the man I marry must love his country first of all, and be able to say to me,

> > "'I could not love thee, dear, so much,
> > Loved I not honor more.'

> "There is no honor above America with me. In this great hour there is no other honor.

> "Your heart will make my words clear to you. I had never expected to say so much, but it has come upon me that I must say the utmost.

> EDITHA"

She thought she had worded her letter well, worded it in a way that could not be bettered; all had been implied and nothing expressed.

She had it ready to send with the packet she had tied with red, white, and blue ribbon, when it occurred to her that she was

　　　　William Dean Howells

not just to him, that she was not giving him a fair chance. He had said he would go and think it over, and she was not waiting. She was pushing, threatening, compelling. That was not a woman's part. She must leave him free, free, free. She could not accept for her country or herself a forced sacrifice.

In writing her letter she had satisfied the impulse from which it sprang; she could well afford to wait till he had thought it over. She put the packet and the letter by, and rested serene in the consciousness of having done what was laid upon her by her love itself to do, and yet used patience, mercy, justice.

She had her reward. Gearson did not come to tea, but she had given him till morning, when, late at night there came up from the village the sound of a fife and drum, with a tumult of voices, in shouting, singing, and laughing. The noise drew nearer and nearer; it reached the street end of the avenue; there it silenced itself, and one voice, the voice she knew best, rose over the silence. It fell; the air was filled with cheers; the fife and drum struck up, with the shouting, singing, and laughing again, but now retreating; and a single figure came hurrying up the avenue.

She ran down to meet her lover and clung to him. He was very gay, and he put his arm round her with a boisterous laugh. "Well, you must call me Captain now; or Cap, if you prefer; that's what the boys call me. Yes, we've had a meeting at the town-hall, and everybody has volunteered; and they selected me for captain, and I'm going to the war, the big war, the glorious war, the holy war ordained by the pocket Providence that blesses butchery. Come along; let's tell the whole family about it. Call them from their downy beds, father, mother, Aunt Hitty, and all the folks!"

But when they mounted the veranda steps he did not wait for a larger  audience; he poured the story out upon Editha alone.

"There was a lot of speaking, and then some of the fools set up a shout for me. It was all going one way, and I thought it would be a good joke to sprinkle a little cold water on them. But you can't do that with a crowd that adores you. The first thing I knew I was sprinkling hell-fire on them. 'Cry havoc, and let slip the dogs of war.' That was the style. Now that it had come to the fight, there were no two parties; there was one country, and the thing was to fight to a finish as quick as possible. I suggested volunteering then and there, and I wrote my name first of all on the roster. Then they elected me— that's all. I wish I had some ice-water."

She left him walking up and down the veranda, while she ran for the ice-pitcher and a goblet, and when she came back he was still walking up and down, shouting the story he had told her to her father and mother, who had come out more sketchily dressed than they commonly were by day. He drank goblet after goblet of the ice-water without noticing who was giving it, and kept on talking, and laughing through his talk wildly. "It's astonishing," he said, "how well the worse reason looks when you try to make it appear the better. Why, I believe I was the first convert to the war in that crowd to-night! I never thought I should like to kill a man; but now I shouldn't care; and the smokeless powder lets you see the man drop that you kill. It's all for the country! What a thing it is to have a country that *can't* be wrong, but if it is, is right, anyway!"

Editha had a great, vital thought, an inspiration. She set down the ice-pitcher on the veranda floor, and ran up-stairs and got the letter she had written him. When at last he noisily bade her father and mother, "Well, goodnight. I forgot I woke you up; I sha'n't want any sleep myself," she followed him down the avenue to the gate. There, after the whirling words that seemed to fly away from her thoughts and refuse to serve them, she made a last effort to solemnize the moment that seemed so crazy, and pressed the letter she had written upon him.

"What's this?" he said. "Want me to mail it?"

"No, no. It's for you. I wrote it after you went this morning.

Keep it—keep it—and read it sometime—" She thought, and then her inspiration came: "Read it if ever you doubt what you've done, or fear that I regret your having done it. Read it after you've started."

They strained each other in embraces that seemed as ineffective as their words, and he kissed her face with quick, hot breaths that were so unlike him, that made her feel as if she had lost her old lover and found a stranger in his place. The stranger said: "What a gorgeous flower you are, with your red hair, and your blue eyes that look black now, and your face with the color painted out by the white moonshine! Let me hold you under the chin, to see whether I love blood, you tiger-lily!" Then he laughed Gearson's laugh, and released her, scared and giddy. Within her wilfulness she had been frightened by a sense of subtler force in him, and mystically mastered as she had never been before.

She ran all the way back to the house, and mounted the steps panting. Her mother and father were talking of the great affair. Her mother said: "Wa'n't Mr. Gearson in rather of an excited state of mind? Didn't you think he acted curious?"

"Well, not for a man who'd just been elected captain and had set 'em up for the whole of Company A," her father chuckled back.

"What in the world do you mean, Mr. Balcom? Oh! There's Editha!" She offered to follow the girl indoors.

"Don't come, mother!" Editha called, vanishing.

Mrs. Balcom remained to reproach her husband. "I don't see much of anything to laugh at."

"Well, it's catching. Caught it from Gearson. I guess it won't be much of a war, and I guess Gearson don't think so, either. The other fellows will back down as soon as they see we mean it. I wouldn't lose any sleep over it. I'm going back to bed, myself."

* * * * *

Gearson came again next afternoon, looking pale and rather sick, but quite himself, even to his languid irony. "I guess I'd better tell you, Editha, that I consecrated myself to your god of battles last night by pouring too many libations to him down my own throat. But I'm all right now. One has to carry off the excitement, somehow."

"Promise me," she commanded, "that you'll never touch it again!"

"What! Not let the cannikin clink? Not let the soldier drink? Well, I promise."

"You don't belong to yourself now; you don't even belong to *me*. You belong to your country, and you have a sacred charge to keep yourself strong and well for your country's sake. I have been thinking, thinking all night and all day long."

"You look as if you had been crying a little, too," he said, with his queer smile.

"That's all past. I've been thinking, and worshipping *you*. Don't you suppose I know all that you've been through, to come to this? I've followed you every step from your old theories and opinions."

"Well, you've had a long row to hoe."

"And I know you've done this from the highest motives—"

"Oh, there won't be much pettifogging to do till this cruel war is—"

"And you haven't simply done it for my sake. I couldn't respect you if you had."

"Well, then we'll say I haven't. A man that hasn't got his own respect intact wants the respect of all the other people he can corner. But we won't go into that. I'm in for the thing now, and we've got to face our future. My idea is that this isn't going to be a very protracted struggle; we shall just scare the enemy to death before it comes to a fight at all. But we must provide for contingencies, Editha. If anything happens to me—"

"Oh, George!" She clung to him, sobbing.

"I don't want you to feel foolishly bound to my memory. I should hate that, wherever I happened to be."

"I am yours, for time and eternity—time and eternity." She liked the words; they satisfied her famine for phrases.

"Well, say eternity; that's all right; but time's another thing; and I'm talking about time. But there is something! My mother! If anything happens—"

She winced, and he laughed. "You're not the bold soldier-girl of yesterday!" Then he sobered. "If anything happens, I want you to help my mother out. She won't like my doing this thing. She brought me up to think war a fool thing as well as a bad thing. My father was in the Civil War; all through it; lost his arm in it." She thrilled with the sense of the arm round her; what if that should be lost? He laughed as if divining her: "Oh, it doesn't run in the family, as far as I know!" Then he added, gravely: "He came home with misgivings about war, and they grew on him. I guess he and mother agreed between them that I was to be brought up in his final mind about it; but that was before my time. I only knew him from my mother's report of him and his opinions; I don't know whether they were hers first; but they were hers last. This will be a blow to her. I shall have to write and tell her—"

He stopped, and she asked: "Would you like me to write, too, George?"

"I don't believe that would do. No, I'll do the writing. She'll understand a little if I say that I thought the way to minimize it was to make war on the largest possible scale at once—that I felt I must have been helping on the war somehow if I hadn't helped keep it from coming, and I knew I hadn't; when it came, I had no right to stay out of it."

Whether his sophistries satisfied him or not, they satisfied her. She clung to his breast, and whispered, with closed eyes and quivering lips: "Yes, yes, yes!"

"But if anything should happen, you might go to her and see what you could do for her. You know? It's rather far off; she can't leave her chair—"

"Oh, I'll go, if it's the ends of the earth! But nothing will happen! Nothing *can*! I—"

She felt herself lifted with his rising, and Gearson was saying, with his arm still round her, to her father: "Well, we're off at once, Mr. Balcom. We're to be formally accepted at the capital, and then bunched up with the rest somehow, and sent into camp somewhere, and got to the front as soon as possible. We all want to be in the van, of course; we're the first company to report to the Governor. I came to tell Editha, but I hadn't got round to it."

\* \* \* \* \*

She saw him again for a moment at the capital, in the station, just before the train started southward with his regiment. He looked well, in his uniform, and very soldierly, but somehow girlish, too, with his clean-shaven face and slim figure. The manly eyes and the strong voice satisfied her, and his preoccupation with some unexpected details of duty flattered her. Other girls were weeping and bemoaning themselves, but she felt a sort of noble distinction in the abstraction, the almost unconsciousness, with which they parted. Only at the last moment he said: "Don't forget my mother. It mayn't be such a walk-over as I supposed," and he laughed at the notion.

He waved his hand to her as the train moved off—she knew it among a score of hands that were waved to other girls from the platform of the car, for it held a letter which she knew was hers. Then he went inside the car to read it, doubtless, and she did not see him again. But she felt safe for him through the strength of what she called her love. What she called her God, always speaking the name in a deep voice and with the implication of a mutual understanding, would watch over him and keep him and bring him back to her. If with an empty sleeve, then he should have three arms instead of two, for both of hers should be his for life. She did not see, though, why she should always be thinking of the arm his father had lost.

There were not many letters from him, but they were such as she could have wished, and she put her whole strength into making hers such as she imagined he could have wished, glorifying and supporting him. She wrote to his mother glorifying him as their hero, but the brief answer she got was merely to the effect that Mrs. Gearson was not well enough to write herself, and thanking her for her letter by the hand of some one who called herself "Yrs truly, Mrs. W. J. Andrews."

Editha determined not to be hurt, but to write again quite as if the answer had been all she expected. Before it seemed as if she could have written, there came news of the first skirmish, and in the list of the killed, which was telegraphed as a trifling loss on our side, was Gearson's name. There was a frantic time of trying to make out that it might be, must be, some other Gearson; but the name and the company and the regiment and the State were too definitely given.

Then there was a lapse into depths out of which it seemed as if she never could rise again; then a lift into clouds far above all grief, black clouds, that blotted out the sun, but where she soared with him, with George—George! She had the fever that she expected of herself, but she did not die in it; she was not even delirious, and it did not last long. When she was well enough to leave her bed, her one thought was of George's mother, of his strangely worded wish that she should go to her and see what she could do for her. In the exaltation of the duty laid upon her—it buoyed her up instead of burdening her—she rapidly recovered.

Her father went with her on the long railroad journey from northern New York to western Iowa; he had business out at Davenport, and he said he could just as well go then as any other time; and he went with her to the little country town where George's mother lived in a little house on the edge of the illimitable cornfields, under trees pushed to a top of the rolling prairie. George's father had settled there after the Civil War, as so many other old soldiers had done; but they were Eastern people, and Editha fancied touches of the East in the June rose overhanging the front door, and the garden with early summer flowers stretching from the gate of the paling fence.

It was very low inside the house, and so dim, with the closed blinds, that they could scarcely see one another: Editha tall and black in her crapes which filled the air with the smell of their dyes; her father standing decorously apart with his hat on his forearm, as at funerals; a woman rested in a deep arm-chair, and the woman who had let the strangers in stood behind the chair.

The seated woman turned her head round and up, and asked the woman behind her chair: "*Who* did you say?"

Editha, if she had done what she expected of herself, would have gone down on her knees at the feet of the seated figure and said, "I am George's Editha," for answer.

But instead of her own voice she heard that other woman's voice, saying: "Well, I don't know as I *did* get the name just right. I guess I'll have to make a little more light in here," and she went and pushed two of the shutters ajar.

William Dean Howells

Then Editha's father said, in his public will-now-address-a-few-remarks tone: "My name is Balcom, ma'am—Junius H. Balcom, of Balcom's Works, New York; my daughter—"

"Oh!" the seated woman broke in, with a powerful voice, the voice that always surprised Editha from Gearson's slender frame. "Let me see you. Stand round where the light can strike on your face," and Editha dumbly obeyed. "So, you're Editha Balcom," she sighed.

"Yes," Editha said, more like a culprit than a comforter.

"What did you come for?" Mrs. Gearson asked.

Editha's face quivered and her knees shook. "I came—because—because George—" She could go no further.

"Yes," the mother said, "he told me he had asked you to come if he got killed. You didn't expect that, I suppose, when you sent him."

"I would rather have died myself than done it!" Editha said, with more truth in her deep voice than she ordinarily found in it. "I tried to leave him free—"

"Yes, that letter of yours, that came back with his other things, left him free."

Editha saw now where George's irony came from.

"It was not to be read before—unless—until—I told him so," she faltered.

"Of course, he wouldn't read a letter of yours, under the circumstances, till he thought you wanted him to. Been sick?" the woman abruptly demanded.

"Very sick," Editha said, with self-pity.

"Daughter's life," her father interposed, "was almost despaired of, at one time."

Mrs. Gearson gave him no heed. "I suppose you would have been glad to die, such a brave person as you! I don't believe *he* was glad to die. He was always a timid boy, that way; he was afraid of a good many things; but if he was afraid he did what he made up his mind to. I suppose he made up his mind to go, but I knew what it cost him by what it cost me when I heard of it. I had been through *one* war before. When you sent him you didn't expect he would get killed."

The voice seemed to compassionate Editha, and it was time. "No," she huskily murmured.

"No, girls don't; women don't, when they give their men up to their country. They think they'll come marching back, somehow, just as gay as they went, or if it's an empty sleeve, or even an empty pantaloon, it's all the more glory, and they're so much the prouder of them, poor things!"

The tears began to run down Editha's face; she had not wept till then; but it was now such a relief to be understood that the tears came.

"No, you didn't expect him to get killed," Mrs. Gearson repeated, in a voice which was startlingly like George's again. "You just expected him to kill some one else, some of those foreigners, that weren't there because they had any say about it, but because they had to be there, poor wretches— conscripts, or whatever they call 'em. You thought it would be all right for my George, *your* George, to kill the sons of those miserable mothers and the husbands of those girls that you would never see the faces of." The woman lifted her powerful voice in a psalmlike note. "I thank my God he didn't live to do it! I thank my God they killed him first, and that he ain't livin' with their blood on his hands!" She dropped her eyes, which she had raised with her voice, and glared at Editha. "What you got that black on for?" She lifted herself by her powerful arms so high that her helpless body seemed to hang limp its full length. "Take it off, take it off, before I tear it from your back!"

* * * * *

The lady who was passing the summer near Balcom's Works was sketching Editha's beauty, which lent itself wonderfully to the effects of a colorist. It had come to that confidence which is rather apt to grow between artist and sitter, and Editha had told her everything.

"To think of your having such a tragedy in your life!" the lady said. She added: "I suppose there are people who feel that way about war. But when you consider the good this war has done —how much it has done for the country! I can't understand such people, for my part. And when you had come all the way out there to console her—got up out of a sick-bed! Well!"

"I think," Editha said, magnanimously, "she wasn't quite in her right mind; and so did papa."

"Yes," the lady said, looking at Editha's lips in nature and then at her lips in art, and giving an empirical touch to them in the picture. "But how dreadful of her! How perfectly—excuse me—how *vulgar!*"

A light broke upon Editha in the darkness which she felt had been without a gleam of brightness for weeks and months. The mystery that had bewildered her was solved by the word; and from that moment she rose from grovelling in shame and self-pity, and began to live again in the ideal.

# VI

## BRAYBRIDGE'S OFFER

We had ordered our dinners and were sitting in the Turkish room at the club, waiting to be called, each in his turn, to the dining-room. It was always a cosey place, whether you found yourself in it with cigars and coffee after dinner, or with whatever liquid or solid appetizer you preferred in the half-hour or more that must pass before dinner after you had made out your menu. It intimated an exclusive possession in the three or four who happened first to find themselves together in it, and it invited the philosophic mind to contemplation more than any other spot in the club.

Our rather limited little down-town dining-club was almost a celibate community at most times. A few husbands and fathers joined us at lunch; but at dinner we were nearly always a company of bachelors, dropping in an hour or so before we wished to dine, and ordering from a bill of fare what we liked. Some dozed away in the intervening time; some read the evening papers or played chess; I preferred the chance society of the Turkish room. I could be pretty sure of finding Wanhope there in these sympathetic moments, and where Wanhope was there would probably be Rulledge, passively willing to listen and agree, and Minver ready to interrupt and dispute. I myself liked to look in and linger for either the reasoning or the bickering, as it happened, and now, seeing the three there together, I took a provisional seat behind the painter, who made no sign of knowing I was present. Rulledge

William Dean Howells

was eating a caviar sandwich, which he had brought from the afternoon tea-table near by, and he greedily incited Wanhope to go on, in the polite pause which the psychologist had let follow on my appearance, with what he was saying. I was not surprised to find that his talk related to a fact just then intensely interesting to the few, rapidly becoming the many, who were privy to it; though Wanhope had the air of stooping to it from a higher range of thinking.

"I shouldn't have supposed, somehow," he said, with a knot of deprecation between his fine eyes, "that he would have had the pluck."

"Perhaps he hadn't," Minver suggested.

Wanhope waited for a thoughtful moment of censure eventuating in toleration. "You mean that she—"

"I don't see why you say that, Minver," Rulledge interposed, chivalrously, with his mouth full of sandwich.

"I didn't say it," Minver contradicted.

"You implied it; and I don't think it's fair. It's easy enough to build up a report of that kind on the half-knowledge of rumor which is all that any outsider can have in the case."

"So far," Minver said, with unbroken tranquillity, "as any such edifice has been erected, you are the architect, Rulledge. I shouldn't think you would like to go round insinuating that sort of thing. Here is Acton," and he now acknowledged my presence with a backward twist of his head, "on the alert for material already. You ought to be more careful where Acton is, Rulledge."

"It would be great copy if it were true," I owned.

Wanhope regarded us all three, in this play of our qualities, with the scientific impartiality of a bacteriologist in the study of a culture offering some peculiar incidents. He took up a point as remote as might be from the personal appeal. "It is curious how little we know of such matters, after all the love-making and marrying in life and all the inquiry of the poets and novelists." He addressed himself in this turn of his thought, half playful, half earnest, to me, as if I united with the functions of both a responsibility for their shortcomings.

"Yes," Minver said, facing about towards me. "How do you excuse yourself for your ignorance in matters where you're always professionally making such a bluff of knowledge? After all the marriages you have brought about in literature, can you say positively and specifically how they are brought about in life?"

"No, I can't," I admitted. "I might say that a writer of fiction is a good deal like a minister who continually marries people without knowing why."

"No, you couldn't, my dear fellow," the painter retorted. "It's part of your swindle to assume that you *do* know why. You ought to find out."

Wanhope interposed concretely, or as concretely as he could: "The important thing would always be to find which of the lovers the confession, tacit or explicit, began with."

"Acton ought to go round and collect human documents bearing on the question. He ought to have got together thousands of specimens from nature. He ought to have gone to all the married couples he knew, and asked them just how their passion was confessed; he ought to have sent out printed circulars, with tabulated questions. Why don't you do it, Acton?"

I returned, as seriously as could have been expected:

"Perhaps it would be thought rather intimate. People don't like to talk of such things."

William Dean Howells

"They're ashamed," Minver declared. "The lovers don't either of them, in a given case, like to let others know how much the woman had to do with making the offer, and how little the man."

Minver's point provoked both Wanhope and myself to begin a remark at the same time. We begged each other's pardon, and Wanhope insisted that I should go on.

"Oh, merely this," I said. "I don't think they're so much ashamed as that they have forgotten the different stages. You were going to say—?"

"Very much what you said. It's astonishing how people forget the vital things and remember trifles. Or perhaps as we advance from stage to stage what once seemed the vital things turn to trifles. Nothing can be more vital in the history of a man and a woman than how they became husband and wife, and yet not merely the details, but the main fact, would seem to escape record if not recollection. The next generations knows nothing of it."

"That appears to let Acton out," Minver said. "But how do *you* know what you were saying, Wanhope?"

"I've ventured to make some inquiries in that region at one time. Not directly, of course. At second and third hand. It isn't inconceivable, if we conceive of a life after this, that a man should forget, in its more important interests and occupations, just how he quitted this world, or at least the particulars of the article of death. Of course, we must suppose a good portion of eternity to have elapsed." Wanhope continued, dreamily, with a deep breath almost equivalent to something so unscientific as a sigh: "Women are charming, and in nothing more than the perpetual challenge they form for us. They are born defying us to match ourselves with them."

"Do you mean that Miss Hazelwood—" Rulledge began, but Minver's laugh arrested him.

"Nothing so concrete, I'm afraid," Wanhope gently returned. "I mean, to match them in graciousness, in loveliness, in all the agile contests of spirit and plays of fancy. It's pathetic to see them caught up into something more serious in that other game, which they are so good at."

"They seem rather to like it, though, some of them, if you mean the game of love," Minver said. "Especially when they're not in earnest about it."

"Oh, there are plenty of spoiled women," Wanhope admitted. "But I don't mean flirting. I suppose that the average unspoiled woman is rather frightened than otherwise when she knows that a man is in love with her."

"Do you suppose she always knows it first?" Rulledge asked.

"You may be sure," Minver answered for Wanhope, "that if she didn't know it, *he* never would." Then Wanhope answered for himself:

"I think that generally she sees it coming. In that sort of wireless telegraphy, that reaching out of two natures through space towards each other, her more sensitive apparatus probably feels the appeal of his before he is conscious of having made any appeal."

"And her first impulse is to escape the appeal?" I suggested.

"Yes," Wanhope admitted, after a thoughtful reluctance.

"Even when she is half aware of having invited it?"

"If she is not spoiled she is never aware of having invited it. Take the case in point; we won't mention any names. She is sailing through time, through youthful space, with her electrical lures, the natural equipment of every charming woman, all out, and suddenly, somewhere from the unknown, she feels the shock of a response in the gulfs of air where there had been no life before. But she can't be said to have knowingly searched the void for any presence."

"Oh, I'm not sure about that, Professor," Minver put in. "Go a little slower, if you expect me to follow you."

"It's all a mystery, the most beautiful mystery of life," Wanhope resumed. "I don't believe I could make out the case as I feel it to be."

"Braybridge's part of the case is rather plain, isn't it?" I invited him.

"I'm not sure of that. No man's part of any case is plain, if you look at it carefully. The most that you can say of Braybridge is that he is rather a simple nature. But nothing," the psychologist added, with one of his deep breaths, "is so complex as a simple nature."

"Well," Minver contended, "Braybridge is plain, if his case isn't."

"Plain? Is he plain?" Wanhope asked, as if asking himself.

"My dear fellow, you agnostics doubt everything!"

"I should have said picturesque. Picturesque, with the sort of unbeautifulness that takes the fancy of women more than Greek proportion. I think it would require a girl peculiarly feminine to feel the attraction of such a man—the fascination of his being grizzled and slovenly and rugged. She would have to be rather a wild, shy girl to do that, and it would have to be through her fear of him that she would divine his fear of her. But what I have heard is that they met under rather exceptional circumstances. It was at a house in the Adirondacks, where Braybridge was, somewhat in the quality of a bull in a china-shop. He was lugged in by the host, as an old friend, and was suffered by the hostess as a friend quite too old for her. At any rate, as I heard (and I don't vouch for the facts, all of them), Braybridge found himself at odds with the gay young people who made up the hostess's end of the party, and was watching for a chance to—"

Wanhope cast about for the word, and Minver supplied it— "Pull out."

"Yes. But when he had found it Miss Hazelwood took it from him."

"I don't understand," Rulledge said.

"When he came in to breakfast, the third morning, prepared with an excuse for cutting his week down to the dimensions it had reached, he saw her sitting alone at the table. She had risen early as a consequence of having arrived late the night before; and when Braybridge found himself in for it, he forgot that he meant to go away, and said good-morning, as if they knew each other. Their hostess found them talking over the length of the table in a sort of mutual fright, and introduced them. But it's rather difficult reporting a lady verbatim at second hand. I really had the facts from Welkin, who had them from his wife. The sum of her impressions was that Braybridge and Miss Hazelwood were getting a kind of comfort out of their mutual terror because one was as badly frightened as the other. It was a novel experience for both. Ever seen her?"

We looked at one another. Minver said: "I never wanted to paint any one so much. It was at the spring show of the American Artists. There was a jam of people; but this girl— I've understood it was she—looked as much alone as if there were nobody else there. She might have been a startled doe in the North Woods suddenly coming out on a twenty-thousand-dollar camp, with a lot of twenty-million-dollar people on the veranda."

"And you wanted to do her as The Startled Doe," I said. "Good selling name."

William Dean Howells

"Don't reduce it to the vulgarity of fiction. I admit it would be a selling name."

"Go on, Wanhope," Rulledge puffed impatiently. "Though I don't see how there could be another soul in the universe as constitutionally scared of men as Braybridge is of women."

"In the universe nothing is wasted, I suppose. Everything has its complement, its response. For every bashful man, there must be a bashful woman," Wanhope returned.

"Or a bold one," Minver suggested.

"No; the response must be in kind to be truly complemental. Through the sense of their reciprocal timidity they divine that they needn't be afraid."

"Oh! *That's* the way you get out of it!"

"Well?" Rulledge urged.

"I'm afraid," Wanhope modestly confessed, "that from this point I shall have to be largely conjectural. Welkin wasn't able to be very definite, except as to moments, and he had his data almost altogether from his wife. Braybridge had told him overnight that he thought of going, and he had said he mustn't think of it; but he supposed Braybridge had spoken of it to Mrs. Welkin, and he began by saying to his wife that he hoped she had refused to hear of Braybridge's going. She said she hadn't heard of it, but now she would refuse without hearing, and she didn't give Braybridge any chance to protest. If people went in the middle of their week, what would become of other people? She was not going to have the equilibrium of her party disturbed, and that was all about it. Welkin thought it was odd that Braybridge didn't insist; and he made a long story of it. But the grain of wheat in his bushel of chaff was that Miss Hazelwood seemed to be fascinated by Braybridge from the first. When Mrs. Welkin scared him into saying that he would stay his week out, the business practically was done. They went picnicking that day in each other's charge; and after Braybridge left he wrote back to her, as Mrs. Welkin knew from the letters that passed through her hands, and—Well, their engagement has come out, and—" Wanhope paused, with an air that was at first indefinite, and then definitive.

"You don't mean," Rulledge burst out in a note of deep wrong, "that that's all you know about it?"

"Yes, that's all I know," Wanhope confessed, as if somewhat surprised himself at the fact.

"Well!"

Wanhope tried to offer the only reparation in his power. "I can conjecture—we can all conjecture—"

He hesitated; then: "Well, go on with your conjecture," Rulledge said, forgivingly.

"Why—" Wanhope began again; but at that moment a man who had been elected the year before, and then gone off on a long absence, put his head in between the dull-red hangings of the doorway. It was Halson, whom I did not know very well, but liked better than I knew. His eyes were dancing with what seemed the inextinguishable gayety of his temperament, rather than any present occasion, and his smile carried his little mustache well away from his handsome teeth. "Private?"

"Come in! come in!" Minver called to him. "Thought you were in Japan?"

"My dear fellow," Halson answered, "you must brush up your contemporary history. It's more than a fortnight since I was in Japan." He shook hands with me, and I introduced him to Rulledge and Wanhope. He said at once: "Well, what is it? Question of Braybridge's engagement? It's humiliating to a man to come back from the antipodes and find the nation absorbed in a parochial problem like that. Everybody I've met

William Dean Howells

here to-night has asked me, the first thing, if I'd heard of it, and if I knew how it could have happened."

"And do you?" Rulledge asked.

"I can give a pretty good guess," Halson said, running his merry eyes over our faces.

"Anybody can give a good guess," Rulledge said. "Wanhope is doing it now."

"Don't let me interrupt." Halson turned to him politely.

"Not at all. I'd rather hear your guess, if you know Braybridge better than I," Wanhope said.

"Well," Halson compromised, "perhaps I've known him longer." He asked, with an effect of coming to business: "Where were you?"

"Tell him, Rulledge," Minver ordered, and Rulledge apparently asked nothing better. He told him, in detail, all we knew from any source, down to the moment of Wanhope's arrested conjecture.

"He did leave you at an anxious point, didn't he?" Halson smiled to the rest of us at Rulledge's expense, and then said: "Well, I think I can help you out a little. Any of you know the lady?"

"By sight, Minver does," Rulledge answered for us. "Wants to paint her."

"Of course," Halson said, with intelligence. "But I doubt if he'd find her as paintable as she looks, at first. She's beautiful, but her charm is spiritual."

"Sometimes we try for that," the painter interposed.

"And sometimes you get it. But you'll allow it's difficult. That's all I meant. I've known her—let me see—for twelve years, at least; ever since I first went West. She was about eleven then, and her father was bringing her up on the ranch. Her aunt came along by and by and took her to Europe—mother dead before Hazelwood went out there. But the girl as always homesick for the ranch; she pined for it; and after they had kept her in Germany three or four years they let her come back and run wild again—wild as a flower does, or a vine, not a domesticated animal."

"Go slow, Halson. This is getting too much for the romantic Rulledge."

"Rulledge can bear up against the facts, I guess, Minver," Halson said, almost austerely. "Her father died two years ago, and then she *had* to come East, for her aunt simply *wouldn't* live on the ranch. She brought her on here, and brought her out; I was at the coming-out tea; but the girl didn't take to the New York thing at all; I could see it from the start; she wanted to get away from it with me, and talk about the ranch."

"She felt that she was with the only genuine person among those conventional people."

Halson laughed at Minver's thrust, and went on amiably: "I don't suppose that till she met Braybridge she was ever quite at her ease with any man—or woman, for that matter. I imagine, as you've done, that it was his fear of her that gave her courage. She met him on equal terms. Isn't that it?"

Wanhope assented to the question referred to him with a nod.

"And when they got lost from the rest of the party at that picnic—"

"Lost?" Rulledge demanded.

"Why, yes. Didn't you know? But I ought to go back. They

said there never was anything prettier than the way she unconsciously went for Braybridge the whole day. She wanted him, and she was a child who wanted things frankly when she did want them. Then his being ten or fifteen years older than she was, and so large and simple, made it natural for a shy girl like her to assort herself with him when all the rest were assorting themselves, as people do at such things. The consensus of testimony is that she did it with the most transparent unconsciousness, and—"

"Who are your authorities?" Minver asked; Rulledge threw himself back on the divan and beat the cushions with impatience.

"Is it essential to give them?"

"Oh no. I merely wondered. Go on."

"The authorities are all right. She had disappeared with him before the others noticed. It was a thing that happened; there was no design in it; that would have been out of character. They had got to the end of the wood-road, and into the thick of the trees where there wasn't even a trail, and they walked round looking for a way out till they were turned completely. They decided that the only way was to keep walking, and by and by they heard the sound of chopping. It was some Canucks clearing a piece of the woods, and when she spoke to them in French they gave them full directions, and Braybridge soon found the path again."

Halson paused, and I said: "But that isn't all?"

"Oh no." He continued thoughtfully silent for a little while before he resumed. "The amazing thing is that they got lost again, and that when they tried going back to the Canucks they couldn't find the way."

"Why didn't they follow the sound of the chopping?" I asked.

"The Canucks had stopped, for the time being. Besides, Braybridge was rather ashamed, and he thought if they went straight on they would be sure to come out somewhere. But that was where he made a mistake. They couldn't go on straight; they went round and round, and came on their own footsteps—or hers, which he recognized from the narrow tread and the dint of the little heels in the damp places."

Wanhope roused himself with a kindling eye. "That is very interesting, the movement in a circle of people who have lost their way. It has often been observed, but I don't know that it has ever been explained. Sometimes the circle is smaller, sometimes it is larger, but I believe it is always a circle."

"Isn't it," I queried, "like any other error in life? We go round and round, and commit the old sins over again."

"That is very interesting," Wanhope allowed.

"But do lost people really always walk in a vicious circle?" Minver asked.

Rulledge would not let Wanhope answer. "Go on, Halson," he said.

Halson roused himself from the revery in which he was sitting with glazed eyes. "Well, what made it a little more anxious was that he had heard of bears on that mountain, and the green afternoon light among the trees was perceptibly paling. He suggested shouting, but she wouldn't let him; she said it would be ridiculous if the others heard them, and useless if they didn't. So they tramped on till—till the accident happened."

"The accident!" Rulledge exclaimed, in the voice of our joint emotion.

"He stepped on a loose stone and turned his foot," Halson explained. "It wasn't a sprain, luckily, but it hurt enough. He turned so white that she noticed it, and asked him what was the matter. Of course that shut his mouth the closer, but it morally doubled his motive, and he kept himself from crying out till the sudden pain of the wrench was over. He said merely that he thought he had heard something, and he had an awful ringing in his ears; but he didn't mean that, and he started on again. The worst was trying to walk without limping, and to talk cheerfully and encouragingly with that agony tearing at him. But he managed somehow, and he was congratulating himself on his success when he tumbled down in a dead faint."

"Oh, come now!" Minver protested.

"It *is* like an old-fashioned story, where things are operated by accident instead of motive, isn't it?" Halson smiled with radiant recognition.

"Fact will always imitate fiction, if you give her time enough," I said.

"Had they got back to the other picnickers?" Rulledge asked, with a tense voice.

"In sound, but not in sight of them. She wasn't going to bring him into camp in that state; besides, she couldn't. She got some water out of the trout-brook they'd been fishing—more water than trout in it—and sprinkled his face, and he came to, and got on his legs just in time to pull on to the others, who were organizing a search-party to go after them. From that point on she dropped Braybridge like a hot coal; and as there was nothing of the flirt in her, she simply kept with the women, the older girls, and the tabbies, and left Braybridge to worry along with the secret of his turned ankle. He doesn't know how he ever got home alive; but he did, somehow, manage to reach the wagons that had brought them to the edge of the woods, and then he was all right till they got to the house. But still she said nothing about his accident, and he couldn't; and he pleaded an early start for town the next morning, and got off to bed as soon as he could."

"I shouldn't have thought he could have stirred in the morning," Rulledge employed Halson's pause to say.

"Well, this beaver *had* to," Halson said. "He was not the only early riser. He found Miss Hazelwood at the station before him."

"What!" Rulledge shouted. I confess the fact rather roused me, too; and Wanhope's eyes kindled with a scientific pleasure.

"She came right towards him. 'Mr. Braybridge,' says she, 'I couldn't let you go without explaining my very strange behavior. I didn't choose to have these people laughing at the notion of *my* having played the part of your preserver. It was bad enough being lost with you; I couldn't bring you into ridicule with them by the disproportion they'd have felt in my efforts for you after you turned your foot. So I simply had to ignore the incident. Don't you see?' Braybridge glanced at her, and he had never felt so big and bulky before, or seen her so slender and little. He said, 'It *would* have seemed rather absurd,' and he broke out and laughed, while she broke down and cried, and asked him to forgive her, and whether it had hurt him very much; and said she knew he could bear to keep it from the others by the way he had kept it from her till he fainted. She implied that he was morally as well as physically gigantic, and it was as much as he could do to keep from taking her in his arms on the spot."

"It would have been edifying to the groom that had driven her to the station," Minver cynically suggested.

"Groom nothing!" Halson returned with spirit. "She paddled herself across the lake, and walked from the boat-landing to the station."

"Jove!" Rulledge exploded in uncontrollable enthusiasm.

"She turned round as soon as she had got through with her hymn of praise—it made Braybridge feel awfully flat—and ran back through the bushes to the boat-landing, and—that was the last he saw of her till he met her in town this fall."

"And when—and when—did he offer himself?" Rulledge entreated, breathlessly. "How—"

"Yes, that's the point, Halson," Minver interposed. "Your story is all very well, as far as it goes; but Rulledge here has been insinuating that it was Miss Hazelwood who made the offer, and he wants you to bear him out."

Rulledge winced at the outrage, but he would not stay Halson's answer even for the sake of righting himself.

"I *have* heard," Minver went on, "that Braybridge insisted on paddling the canoe back to the other shore for her, and that it was on the way that he offered himself." We others stared at Minver in astonishment. Halson glanced covertly towards him with his gay eyes. "Then that wasn't true?"

"How did you hear it?" Halson asked.

"Oh, never mind. Is it true?"

"Well, I know there's that version," Halson said, evasively. "The engagement is only just out, as you know. As to the offer—the when and the how—I don't know that I'm exactly at liberty to say."

"I don't see why," Minver urged. "You might stretch a point for Rulledge's sake."

Halson looked down, and then he glanced at Minver after a furtive passage of his eye over Rulledge's intense face. "There was something rather nice happened after—But, really, now!"

"Oh, go on!" Minver called out in contempt of his scruple.

"I haven't the right—Well, I suppose I'm on safe ground here?

It won't go any further, of course; and it *was* so pretty! After she had pushed off in her canoe, you know, Braybridge—he'd followed her down to the shore of the lake—found her handkerchief in a bush where it had caught, and he held it up, and called out to her. She looked round and saw it, and called back: 'Never mind. I can't return for it now.' Then Braybridge plucked up his courage, and asked if he might keep it, and she said 'Yes,' over her shoulder, and then she stopped paddling, and said: 'No, no, you mustn't, you mustn't! You can send it to me.' He asked where, and she said: 'In New York—in the fall—at the Walholland.' Braybridge never knew how he dared, but he shouted after her—she was paddling on again— 'May I *bring* it?' and she called over her shoulder again, without fully facing him, but her profile was enough: 'If you can't get any one to bring it for you.' The words barely reached him, but he'd have caught them if they'd been whispered; and he watched her across the lake and into the bushes, and then broke for his train. He was just in time."

Halson beamed for pleasure upon us, and even Minver said: "Yes, that's rather nice." After a moment he added: "Rulledge thinks she put it there."

"You're too bad, Minver," Halson protested. "The charm of the whole thing was her perfect innocence. She isn't capable of the slightest finesse. I've known her from a child, and I know what I say."

"That innocence of girlhood," Wanhope said, "is very interesting. It's astonishing how much experience it survives. Some women carry it into old age with them. It's never been scientifically studied—"

"Yes," Minver allowed. "There would be a fortune for the novelist who could work a type of innocence for all it was worth. Here's Acton always dealing with the most rancid flirtatiousness, and missing the sweetness and beauty of a girlhood which does the cheekiest things without knowing what it's about, and fetches down its game whenever it shuts its eyes and fires at nothing. But I don't see how all this touches the point that Rulledge makes, or decides which finally made the offer."

"Well, hadn't the offer already been made?"

"But how?"

"Oh, in the usual way."

"What is the usual way?"

"I thought everybody knew *that*. Of course, it was *from* Braybridge finally, but I suppose it's always six of one and half a dozen of the other in these cases, isn't it? I dare say he couldn't get any one to take her the handkerchief. My dinner?" Halson looked up at the silent waiter, who had stolen upon us and was bowing towards him.

"Look here, Halson," Minver detained him, "how is it none of the rest of us have heard all those details?"

"*I* don't know where you've been, Minver. Everybody knows the main facts," Halson said, escaping.

Wanhope observed, musingly: "I suppose he's quite right about the reciprocality of the offer, as we call it. There's probably, in ninety-nine cases out of a hundred, a perfect understanding before there's an explanation. In many cases the offer and the acceptance must really be tacit."

"Yes," I ventured, "and I don't know why we're so severe with women when they seem to take the initiative. It's merely, after all, the call of the maiden bird, and there's nothing lovelier or more endearing in nature than that."

"Maiden bird is good, Acton," Minver approved. "Why don't you institute a class of fiction where the love-making is all done by the maiden birds, as you call them—or the widow birds? It would be tremendously popular with both sexes. It would lift an immense responsibility off the birds who've been expected to shoulder it heretofore if it could be introduced into real life."

Rulledge fetched a long, simple-hearted sigh. "Well, it's a charming story. How well he told it!"

The waiter came again, and this time signalled to Minver.

"Yes," he said, as he rose. "What a pity you can't believe a word Halson says."

"Do you mean—" we began simultaneously.

"That he built the whole thing from the ground up, with the start that we had given him. Why, you poor things! Who could have told him how it all happened? Braybridge? Or the girl? As Wanhope began by saying, people don't speak of their love-making, even when they distinctly remember it."

"Yes, but see here, Minver!" Rulledge said, with a dazed look. "If it's all a fake of his, how came *you* to have heard of Braybridge paddling the canoe back for her?"

"That was the fake that tested the fake. When he adopted it, I *knew* he was lying, because I was lying myself. And then the cheapness of the whole thing! I wonder that didn't strike you. It's the stuff that a thousand summer-girl stories have been spun out of. Acton might have thought he was writing it!"

He went away, leaving us to a blank silence, till Wanhope managed to say: "That inventive habit of mind is very curious. It would be interesting to know just how far it imposes on the inventor himself—how much he believes of his own fiction."

"I don't see," Rulledge said, gloomily, "why they're so long

William Dean Howells

with my dinner." Then he burst out: "I believe every word Halson said! If there's any fake in the thing, it's the fake that Minver owned to."

VII

## THE CHICK OF THE EASTER EGG

The old fellow who told that story of dream-transference on a sleeping-car at Christmas-time was again at the club on Easter Eve. Halson had put him up for the winter, under the easy rule we had, and he had taken very naturally to the Turkish room for his after-dinner coffee and cigar. We all rather liked him, though it was Minver's pose to be critical of the simple friendliness with which he made himself at home among us, and to feign a wish that there were fewer trains between Boston and New York, so that old Newton (that was his name) could have a better chance of staying away. But we noticed that Minver was always a willing listener to Newton's talk, and that he sometimes hospitably offered to share his tobacco with the Bostonian. When brought to book for his inconsistency by Rulledge, he said he was merely welcoming the new blood, if not young blood, that Newton was infusing into our body, which had grown anaemic on Wanhope's psychology and Rulledge's romance; or, anyway, it was a change.

Newton now began by saying abruptly, in a fashion he had, "We used to hear a good deal in Boston about your Easter Parade here in New York. Do you still keep it up?"

No one else answering, Minver replied, presently, "I believe it is still going on. I understand that it's composed mostly of milliners out to see one another's new hats, and generous Jewesses who are willing to contribute the 'dark and bright' of

William Dean Howells

the beauty in which they walk to the observance of an alien faith. It's rather astonishing how the synagogue takes to the feasts of the church. If it were not for that, I don't know what would become of Christmas."

"What do you mean by their walking in beauty?" Rulledge asked over his shoulder.

"I shall never have the measure of your ignorance, Rulledge. You don't even know Byron's lines on Hebrew loveliness?

"She walks in beauty like the night
Of cloudless climes and starry skies,
And all that's best of dark and bright
Meets in her aspect and her eyes."

"Pretty good," Rulledge assented. "And they *are* splendid, sometimes. But what has the Easter Parade got to do with it?" he asked Newton.

"Oh, only what everything has with everything else. I was thinking of Easter-time long ago and far away, and naturally I thought of Easter now and here. I saw your Parade once, and it seemed to me one of the great social spectacles. But you can't keep anything in New York, if it's good; if it's bad, you can."

"You come from Boston, I think you said, Mr. Newton," Minver breathed blandly through his smoke.

"Oh, I'm not a *real* Bostonian," our guest replied. "I'm not abusing you on behalf of a city that I'm a native proprietor of. If I were, I shouldn't perhaps make your decadent Easter Parade my point of attack, though I think it's a pity to let it spoil. I came from a part of the country where we used to make a great deal of Easter, when we were boys, at least so far as eggs went. I don't know whether the grown people observed the day then, and I don't know whether the boys keep it now; I haven't been back at Easter-time for several generations. But when I was a boy it was a serious thing. In that soft

Southwestern latitude the grass had pretty well greened up by Easter, even when it came in March, and grass colors eggs a very nice yellow; it used to worry me that it didn't color them green. When the grass hadn't got along far enough, winter wheat would do as well. I don't remember what color onion husks would give; but we used onion husks, too. Some mothers would let the boys get logwood from the drug-store, and that made the eggs a fine, bold purplish black. But the greatest egg of all was a calico egg, that you got by coaxing your grandmother (your mother's mother) or your aunt (your mother's sister) to sew up in a tight cover of brilliant calico. When that was boiled long enough the colors came off in a perfect pattern on the egg. Very few boys could get such eggs; when they did, they put them away in bureau drawers till they ripened and the mothers smelt them, and threw them out of the window as quickly as possible. Always, after breakfast, Easter Morning, we came out on the street and fought eggs. We pitted the little ends of the eggs against one another, and the fellow whose egg cracked the other fellow's egg won it, and he carried it off. I remember grass and wheat colored eggs in such trials of strength, and onion and logwood colored eggs; but never calico eggs; *they* were too precious to be risked; it would have seemed wicked.

"I don't know," the Boston man went musingly on, "why I should remember these things so relentlessly; I've forgotten all the important things that happened to me then; but perhaps these were the important things. Who knows? I only know I've always had a soft spot in my heart for Easter, not so much because of the calico eggs, perhaps, as because of the grandmothers and the aunts. I suppose the simple life is full of such aunts and grandmothers still; but you don't find them in hotel apartments, or even in flats consisting of seven large, light rooms and bath." We all recognized the language of the advertisements, and laughed in sympathy with our guest, who perhaps laughed out of proportion with a pleasantry of that size.

When he had subdued his mirth, he resumed at a point

William Dean Howells

apparently very remote from that where he had started.

"There was one of those winters in Cambridge, where I lived then, that seemed tougher than any other we could remember, and they were all pretty tough winters there in those times. There were forty snowfalls between Thanksgiving and Fast Day—you don't know what Fast Day is in New York, and we didn't, either, as far as the fasting went—and the cold kept on and on till we couldn't, or said we couldn't, stand it any longer. So, along about the middle of March somewhere, we picked up the children and started south. In those days New York seemed pretty far south to us; and when we got here we found everything on wheels that we had left on runners in Boston. But the next day it began to snow, and we said we must go a little farther to meet the spring. I don't know exactly what it was made us pitch on Bethlehem, Pennsylvania; but we had a notion we should find it interesting, and, at any rate, a total change from our old environment. We had been reading something about the Moravians, and we knew that it was the capital of Moravianism, with the largest Moravian congregation in the world; I think it was Longfellow's 'Hymn of the Moravian Nuns' that set us to reading about the sect; and we had somehow heard that the Sun Inn, at Bethlehem, was the finest old-fashioned public house anywhere. At any rate, we had the faith of our youthful years, and we put out for Bethlehem."

"We arrived just at dusk, but not so late that we couldn't see the hospitable figure of a man coming out of the Sun to meet us at the omnibus door and to shake hands with each of us. It was the very pleasantest and sweetest welcome we ever had at a public house; and though we found the Sun a large, modern hotel, we easily accepted the landlord's assurance that the old Inn was built up inside of the hotel, just as it was when Washington stayed in it; and after a mighty good supper we went to our rooms, which were piping warm from two good base-burner stoves. It was not exactly the vernal air we had expected of Bethlehem when we left New York; but you can't have everything in this world, and, with the snowbanks along the streets outside, we were very glad to have the base-burners."

"We went to bed pretty early, and I fell into one of those exemplary sleeps that begin with no margin of waking after your head touches the pillow, or before that, even, and I woke from a dream of heavenly music that translated itself into the earthly notes of bugles. It made me sit up with the instant realization that we had arrived in Bethlehem on Easter Eve, and that this was Easter Morning. We had read of the beautiful observance of the feast by the Moravians, and, while I was hurrying on my clothes beside my faithful base-burner, I kept quite superfluously wondering at myself for not having thought of it, and so made sure of being called. I had waked just in time, though I hadn't deserved to do so, and ought, by right, to have missed it all. I tried to make my wife come with me; but after the family is of a certain size a woman, if she is a real woman, thinks her husband can see things for her, and generally sends him out to reconnoitre and report. Besides, my wife couldn't have left the children without waking them, to tell them she was going, and then all five of them would have wanted to come with us, including the baby; and we should have had no end of a time convincing them of the impossibility. We were a good deal bound up in the children, and we hated to lie to them when we could possibly avoid it. So I went alone."

"I asked the night porter, who was still on duty, the way I wanted to take, but there were so many people in the streets going the same direction that I couldn't have missed it, anyhow; and pretty soon we came to the old Moravian cemetery, which was in the heart of the town; and there we found most of the Moravian congregation drawn up on three sides of the square, waiting and facing the east, which was beginning to redden. Of all the cemeteries I have seen, that was the most beautiful, because it was the simplest and humblest. Generally a cemetery is a dreadful place, with headstones and footstones and shafts and tombs scattered about, and looking like a field full of granite and marble stumps from the clearing of a petrified forest. But here all the

William Dean Howells

memorial tablets lay flat with the earth. None of the dead were assumed to be worthier of remembrance than another; they all rested at regular intervals, with their tablets on their breasts, like shields, in their sleep after the battle of life. I was thinking how right and wise this was, and feeling the purity of the conception like a quality of the keen, clear air of the morning, which seemed to be breathing straight from the sky, when suddenly the sun blazed up from the horizon like a fire, and the instant it appeared the horns of the band began to blow and the people burst into a hymn—a thousand voices, for all I know. It was the sublimest thing I ever heard, and I don't know that there's anything to match it for dignity and solemnity in any religious rite. It made the tears come, for I thought how those people were of a church of missionaries and martyrs from the beginning, and I felt as if I were standing in sight and hearing of the first Christians after Christ. It was as if He were risen there 'in the midst of them.'"

Rulledge looked round on the rest of us, with an air of acquiring merit from the Bostonian's poetry, but Minver's gravity was proof against the chance of mocking Rulledge, and I think we all felt alike. Wanhope seemed especially interested, though he said nothing.

"When I went home I told my wife about it as well as I could, but, though she entered into the spirit of it, she was rather preoccupied. The children had all wakened, as they did sometimes, in a body, and were storming joyfully around the rooms, as if it were Christmas; and she was trying to get them dressed. 'Do tell them what Easter is like; they've never seen it kept before,' she said; and I tried to do so, while I took a hand, as a young father will, and tried to get them into their clothes. I don't think I dwelt much on the religious observance of the day, but I dug up some of my profane associations with it in early life, and told them about coloring eggs, and fighting them, and all that; there in New England, in those days, they had never seen or heard of such a thing as an Easter egg."

"I don't think my reminiscences quieted them much. They

were all on fire—the oldest hoy and girl, and the twins, and even the two-year-old that we called the baby—to go out and buy some eggs and get the landlord to let them color them in the hotel kitchen. I had a deal of ado to make them wait till after breakfast, but I managed, somehow; and when we had finished—it was a mighty good Pennsylvania breakfast, such as we could eat with impunity in those halcyon days: rich coffee, steak, sausage, eggs, applebutter, buckwheat cakes and maple syrup—we got their out-door togs on them, while they were all stamping and shouting round and had to be caught and overcoated, and fur-capped and hooded simultaneously, and managed to get them into the street together. Ever been in Bethlehem?"

We all had to own our neglect of this piece of travel; and Newton, after a moment of silent forgiveness, said:

"Well, I don't know how it is now, but twenty-five or thirty years ago it was the most interesting town in America. It wasn't the old Moravian community that it had been twenty-five years before that, when none but Moravians could buy property there; but it was like the Sun Hotel, and just as that had grown round and over the old Sun Inn, the prosperous manufacturing town, with its iron-foundries and zinc-foundries, and all the rest of it, had grown round and over the original Moravian village. If you wanted a breath of perfect strangeness, with an American quality in it at the same time, you couldn't have gone to any place where you could have had it on such terms as you could in Bethlehem. I can't begin to go into details, but one thing was hearing German spoken everywhere in the street: not the German of Germany, but the Pennsylvania German, with its broad vowels and broken-down grammatical forms, and its English vocables and interjections, which you caught in the sentences which came to you, like *av coorse*, and *yes* and *no* for *ja* and *nein*. There were stores where they spoke no English, and others where they made a specialty of it; and I suppose when we sallied out that bright Sunday morning, with the baby holding onto a hand of each of us between us, and the twins going in front with their brother and sister, we were almost as foreign as we should have been in a village on the Rhine or the Elbe."

"We got a little acquainted with the people, after awhile, and I heard some stories of the country folks that I thought were pretty good. One was about an old German farmer on whose land a prospecting metallurgist found zinc ore; the scientific man brought him the bright yellow button by which the zinc proved its existence in its union with copper, and the old fellow asked in an awestricken whisper: 'Is it a gold-mine?' 'No, no. Guess again.' 'Then it's a *brass-mine*!' But before they began to find zinc there in the lovely Lehigh Valley—you can stand by an open zinc-mine and look down into it where the rock and earth are left standing, and you seem to be looking down into a range of sharp mountain peaks and pinnacles—it was the richest farming region in the whole fat State of Pennsylvania; and there was a young farmer who owned a vast tract of it, and who went to fetch home a young wife from Philadelphia way, somewhere. He drove there and back in his own buggy, and when he reached the top overlooking the valley, with his bride, he stopped his horse, and pointed with his whip. 'There,' he said, 'as far as the sky is blue, it's all ours!' I thought that was fine."

"Fine?" I couldn't help bursting out; "it's a stroke of poetry."

Minver cut in: "The thrifty Acton making a note of it for future use in literature."

"Eh!" Newton queried. "Oh! I don't mind. You're welcome to it, Mr. Acton. It's a pity somebody shouldn't use it, and of course *I* can't."

"Acton will send you a copy with the usual forty-per-cent. discount and ten off for cash," the painter said.

They had their little laugh at my expense, and then Newton took up his tale again. "Well, as I was saying—By the way, what *was* I saying?"

The story-loving Rulledge remembered. "You went out with your wife and children for Easter eggs."

"Oh yes. Thank you. Well, of course, in a town geographically American, the shops were all shut on Sunday, and we couldn't buy even an Easter egg on Easter Sunday. But one of the stores had the shade of its show-window up, and the children simply glued themselves to it in such a fascination that we could hardly unstick them. That window was full of all kinds of Easter things—I don't remember what all; but there were Easter eggs in every imaginable color and pattern, and besides these there were whole troops of toy rabbits. I had forgotten that the natural offspring of Easter eggs is rabbits; but I took a brace, and remembered the fact and announced it to the children. They immediately demanded an explanation, with all sorts of scientific particulars, which I gave them, as reckless of the truth as I thought my wife would suffer without contradicting me. I had to say that while Easter eggs mostly hatched rabbits, there were instances in which they hatched other things, as, for instance, handfuls of eagles and half-eagles and double-eagles, especially in the case of the golden eggs that the goose laid. They knew all about that goose; but I had to tell them what those unfamiliar pieces of American coinage were, and promise to give them one each when they grew up, if they were good. That only partially satisfied them, and they wanted to know specifically what other kinds of things Easter eggs would hatch if properly treated. Each one had a preference; the baby always preferred what the last one said; and *she* wanted an ostrich, the same as her big brother; he was seven then."

"I don't really know how we lived through the day; I mean the children, for my wife and I went to the Moravian church, and had a good long Sunday nap in the afternoon, while the children were pining for Monday morning, when they could buy eggs and begin to color them, so that they could hatch just the right kind of Easter things. When I woke up I had to fall in with a theory they had agreed to between them that any kind of two-legged or four-legged chick that hatched from an Easter egg would wear the same color, or the same kind of spots or

William Dean Howells

stripes, that the egg had."

"I found that they had arranged to have calico eggs, and they were going to have their mother cover them with the same sort of cotton prints that I had said my grandmother and aunts used, and they meant to buy the calico in the morning at the same time that they bought the eggs. We had some tin vessels of water on our stoves to take the dryness out of the hot air, and they had decided that they would boil their eggs in these, and not trouble the landlord for the use of his kitchen."

"There was nothing in this scheme wanting but their mother's consent—I agreed to it on the spot—but when she understood that they each expected to have two eggs apiece, with one apiece for us, she said she never could cover a dozen eggs in the world, and that the only way would be for them to go in the morning with us, and choose each the handsomest egg they could out of the eggs in that shop-window. They met this proposition rather blankly at first; but on reflection the big brother said it would be a shame to spoil mamma's Easter by making her work all day, and besides it would keep till that night, anyway, before they could begin to have any fun with their eggs; and then the rest all said the same thing, ending with the baby: and accepted the inevitable with joy, and set about living through the day as well as they could."

"They had us up pretty early the next morning—that is, they had me up; their mother said that I had brought it on myself, and richly deserved it for exciting their imaginations, and I had to go out with the two oldest and the twins to choose the eggs; we got off from the baby by promising to let her have two, and she didn't understand very well, anyway, and was awfully sleepy. We were a pretty long time choosing the six eggs, and I don't remember now just what they were; but they were certainly joyous eggs; and—By the way, I don't know why I'm boring a brand of hardened bachelors like you with all these domestic details?"

"Oh, don't mind *us*," Minver responded to his general appeal.

"We may not understand the feelings of a father, but we are all mothers at heart, especially Rulledge. Go on. It's very exciting," he urged, not very ironically, and Newton went on.

"Well, I don't believe I could say just how the havoc began. They put away their eggs very carefully after they had made their mother admire them, and shown the baby how hers were the prettiest, and they each said in succession that they must be very precious of them, for if you shook an egg, or anything, it wouldn't hatch; and it was their plan to take these home and set an unemployed pullet, belonging to the big brother, to hatching them in the coop that he had built of laths for her in the back yard with his own hands. But long before the afternoon was over, the evil one had entered Eden, and tempted the boy to try fighting eggs with these treasured specimens, as I had told we boys used to fight eggs in my town in the southwest. He held a conquering course through the encounter with three eggs, but met his Waterloo with a regular Bluecher belonging to the baby. Then he instantly changed sides; and smashed his Bluecher against the last egg left. By that time all the other children were in tears, the baby roaring powerfully in ignorant sympathy, and the victor steeped in silent gloom. His mother made him gather up the ruins from the floor, and put them in the stove, and she took possession of the victorious egg, and said she would keep it till we got back to Cambridge herself, and not let one of them touch it. I can tell you it was a tragical time. I wanted to go out and buy them another set of eggs, and spring them for a surprise on them in the morning, after they had suffered enough that night. But she said that if I dared to dream of such a thing— which would be the ruin of the children's character, by taking away the consequences of their folly—she should do, she did not know what, to me. Of course she was right, and I gave in, and helped the children forget all about it, so that by the time we got back to Cambridge I had forgotten about it myself."

"I don't know what it was reminded the boy of that remaining Easter egg unless it was the sight of the unemployed pullet in her coop, which he visited the first thing; and I don't know

William Dean Howells

how he managed to wheedle his mother out of it; but the first night after I came home from business—it was rather late and the children had gone to bed—she told me that ridiculous boy, as she called him in self-exculpation, had actually put the egg under his pullet, and all the children were wild to see what it would hatch. 'And now,' she said, severely, 'what are you going to do? You have filled their heads with those ideas, and I suppose you will have to invent some nonsense or other to fool them, and make them believe that it has hatched a giraffe, or an elephant, or something; they won't be satisfied with anything less.' I said we should have to try something smaller, for I didn't think we could manage a chick of that size on our lot; and that I should trust in Providence. Then she said it was all very well to laugh; and that I couldn't get out of it that way, and I needn't think it."

"I didn't, much. But the children understood that it took three weeks for an egg to hatch, and anyway the pullet was so intermittent in her attentions to the Easter egg, only sitting on it at night, or when held down by hand in the day, that there was plenty of time. One evening when I came out from Boston, I was met by a doleful deputation at the front gate, with the news that when the coop was visited that morning after breakfast—they visited the coop every morning before they went to school—the pullet was found perched on a cross-bar in a high state of nerves, and the shell of the Easter egg broken and entirely eaten out. Probably a rat had got in and done it, or, more hopefully, a mink, such as used to attack eggs in the town where I was a boy. We went out and viewed the wreck, as a first step towards a better situation; and suddenly a thought struck me. 'Children,' I said, 'what did you really expect that egg to hatch, anyway?' They looked askance at one another, and at last the boy said: 'Well, you know, papa, an egg that's been cooked—' And then we all laughed together, and I knew they had been making believe as much as I had, and no more expected the impossible of a boiled egg than I did."

"That was charming!" Wanhope broke out. "There is nothing

more interesting than the way children join in hypnotizing themselves with the illusions which their parents think *they* have created without their help. In fact, it is very doubtful whether at any age we have any illusions except those of our own creation; we—"

"Let him go on, Wanhope," Minver dictated; and Newton continued.

"It was rather nice. I asked them if their mother knew about the egg; and they said that of course they couldn't help telling her; and I said: 'Well, then, I'll tell you what: we must make her believe that the chick hatched out and got away—' The boy stopped me: 'Do you think that would be exactly true, papa?' 'Well, not *exactly* true; but it's only for the time being. We can tell her the exact truth afterwards,' and then I laid my plan before them. They said it was perfectly splendid, and would be the greatest kind of joke on mamma, and one that she would like as much as anybody. The thing was to keep it from her till it was done, and they all promised that they wouldn't tell; but I could see that they were bursting with the secret the whole evening."

"The next day was Saturday, when I always went home early, and I had the two oldest children come in with the second-girl, who left them to take lunch with me. They had chocolate and ice-cream, and after lunch we went around to a milliner's shop in West Street, where my wife and I had stopped a long five minutes the week before we went to Bethlehem, adoring an Easter bonnet that we saw in the window. I wanted her to buy it; but she said, No, if we were going that expensive journey, we couldn't afford it, and she must do without, that spring. I showed it to them, and 'Now, children,' I said, 'what do you think of that for the chick that your Easter egg hatched?' And they said it was the most beautiful bonnet they had ever seen, and it would just exactly suit mamma. But I saw they were holding something back, and I said, sharply, 'Well?' and they both guiltily faltered out: 'The *bird*, you know, papa,' and I remembered that they belonged to the society of Bird

William Dean Howells

Defenders, who in that day were pledged against the decorative use of dead birds or killing them for anything but food. 'Why, confound it,' I said, 'the bird is the very thing that makes it an Easter-egg chick!' but I saw that their honest little hearts were troubled, and I said again: 'Confound it! Let's go in and hear what the milliner has to say.' Well, the long and short of it was that the milliner tried a bunch of forget-me-nots over the bluebird that we all agreed was a thousand times better, and that if it were substituted would only cost three dollars more, and we took our Easter-egg chick home in a blaze of glory, the children carrying the bandbox by the string between them."

"Of course we had a great time opening it, and their mother acted her part so well that I knew she was acting, and after the little ones were in bed I taxed her with it. 'Know? Of course I knew!' she said. 'Did you think they would let you *deceive* me? They're true New-Englanders, and they told me all about it last night, when I was saying their prayers with them.' 'Well,' I said, 'they let you deceive *me*; they must be true Westerners, too, for they didn't tell me a word of your knowing.' I rather had her there, but she said: 'Oh, you goose—' We were young people in those days, and goose meant everything. But, really, I'm ashamed of getting off all this to you hardened bachelors, as I said before—"

"If you tell many more such stories in this club," Minver said, severely, "you won't leave a bachelor in it. And Rulledge will be the first to get married."

THE END

# Choose from Thousands of 1stWorldLibrary Classics By

A. M. Barnard
Ada Leverson
Adolphus William Ward
Aesop
Agatha Christie
Alexander Aaronsohn
Alexander Kielland
Alexandre Dumas
Alfred Gatty
Alfred Ollivant
Alice Duer Miller
Alice Turner Curtis
Alice Dunbar
Allen Chapman
Alleyne Ireland
Ambrose Bierce
Amelia E. Barr
Amory H. Bradford
Andrew Lang
Andrew McFarland Davis
Andy Adams
Angela Brazil
Anna Alice Chapin
Anna Sewell
Annie Besant
Annie Hamilton Donnell
Annie Payson Call
Annie Roe Carr
Annonaymous
Anton Chekhov
Archibald Lee Fletcher
Arnold Bennett
Arthur C. Benson
Arthur Conan Doyle
Arthur M. Winfield
Arthur Ransome
Arthur Schnitzler
Arthur Train
Atticus
B.H. Baden-Powell
B. M. Bower
B. C. Chatterjee
Baroness Emmuska Orczy
Baroness Orczy
Basil King
Bayard Taylor
Ben Macomber
Bertha Muzzy Bower
Bjornstjerne Bjornson

Booth Tarkington
Boyd Cable
Bram Stoker
C. Collodi
C. E. Orr
C. M. Ingleby
Carolyn Wells
Catherine Parr Traill
Charles A. Eastman
Charles Amory Beach
Charles Dickens
Charles Dudley Warner
Charles Farrar Browne
Charles Ives
Charles Kingsley
Charles Klein
Charles Hanson Towne
Charles Lathrop Pack
Charles Romyn Dake
Charles Whibley
Charles Willing Beale
Charlotte M. Braeme
Charlotte M. Yonge
Charlotte Perkins Stetson
Clair W. Hayes
Clarence Day Jr.
Clarence E. Mulford
Clemence Housman
Confucius
Coningsby Dawson
Cornelis DeWitt Wilcox
Cyril Burleigh
D. H. Lawrence
Daniel Defoe
David Garnett
Dinah Craik
Don Carlos Janes
Donald Keyhoe
Dorothy Kilner
Dougan Clark
Douglas Fairbanks
E. Nesbit
E. P. Roe
E. Phillips Oppenheim
E. S. Brooks
Earl Barnes
Edgar Rice Burroughs
Edith Van Dyne
Edith Wharton

Edward Everett Hale
Edward J. O'Biren
Edward S. Ellis
Edwin L. Arnold
Eleanor Atkins
Eleanor Hallowell Abbott
Eliot Gregory
Elizabeth Gaskell
Elizabeth McCracken
Elizabeth Von Arnim
Ellem Key
Emerson Hough
Emilie F. Carlen
Emily Bronte
Emily Dickinson
Enid Bagnold
Enilor Macartney Lane
Erasmus W. Jones
Ernie Howard Pie
Ethel May Dell
Ethel Turner
Ethel Watts Mumford
Eugene Sue
Eugenie Foa
Eugene Wood
Eustace Hale Ball
Evelyn Everett-green
Everard Cotes
F. H. Cheley
F. J. Cross
F. Marion Crawford
Fannie E. Newberry
Federick Austin Ogg
Ferdinand Ossendowski
Fergus Hume
Florence A. Kilpatrick
Fremont B. Deering
Francis Bacon
Francis Darwin
Frances Hodgson Burnett
Frances Parkinson Keyes
Frank Gee Patchin
Frank Harris
Frank Jewett Mather
Frank L. Packard
Frank V. Webster
Frederic Stewart Isham
Frederick Trevor Hill
Frederick Winslow Taylor

Friedrich Kerst
Friedrich Nietzsche
Fyodor Dostoyevsky
G.A. Henty
G.K. Chesterton
Gabrielle E. Jackson
Garrett P. Serviss
Gaston Leroux
George A. Warren
George Ade
Geroge Bernard Shaw
George Cary Eggleston
George Durston
George Ebers
George Eliot
George Gissing
George MacDonald
George Meredith
George Orwell
George Sylvester Viereck
George Tucker
George W. Cable
George Wharton James
Gertrude Atherton
Gordon Casserly
Grace E. King
Grace Gallatin
Grace Greenwood
Grant Allen
Guillermo A. Sherwell
Gulielma Zollinger
Gustav Flaubert
H. A. Cody
H. B. Irving
H.C. Bailey
H. G. Wells
H. H. Munro
H. Irving Hancock
H. R. Naylor
H. Rider Haggard
H. W. C. Davis
Haldeman Julius
Hall Caine
Hamilton Wright Mabie
Hans Christian Andersen
Harold Avery
Harold McGrath
Harriet Beecher Stowe
Harry Castlemon
Harry Coghill
Harry Houidini

Hayden Carruth
Helent Hunt Jackson
Helen Nicolay
Hendrik Conscience
Hendy David Thoreau
Henri Barbusse
Henrik Ibsen
Henry Adams
Henry Ford
Henry Frost
Henry James
Henry Jones Ford
Henry Seton Merriman
Henry W Longfellow
Herbert A. Giles
Herbert Carter
Herbert N. Casson
Herman Hesse
Hildegard G. Frey
Homer
Honore De Balzac
Horace B. Day
Horace Walpole
Horatio Alger Jr.
Howard Pyle
Howard R. Garis
Hugh Lofting
Hugh Walpole
Humphry Ward
Ian Maclaren
Inez Haynes Gillmore
Irving Bacheller
Isabel Cecilia Williams
Isabel Hornibrook
Israel Abrahams
Ivan Turgenev
J.G.Austin
J. Henri Fabre
J. M. Barrie
J. M. Walsh
J. Macdonald Oxley
J. R. Miller
J. S. Fletcher
J. S. Knowles
J. Storer Clouston
J. W. Duffield
Jack London
Jacob Abbott
James Allen
James Andrews
James Baldwin

James Branch Cabell
James DeMille
James Joyce
James Lane Allen
James Lane Allen
James Oliver Curwood
James Oppenheim
James Otis
James R. Driscoll
Jane Abbott
Jane Austen
Jane L. Stewart
Janet Aldridge
Jens Peter Jacobsen
Jerome K. Jerome
Jessie Graham Flower
John Buchan
John Burroughs
John Cournos
John F. Kennedy
John Gay
John Glasworthy
John Habberton
John Joy Bell
John Kendrick Bangs
John Milton
John Philip Sousa
John Taintor Foote
Jonas Lauritz Idemil Lie
Jonathan Swift
Joseph A. Altsheler
Joseph Carey
Joseph Conrad
Joseph E. Badger Jr
Joseph Hergesheimer
Joseph Jacobs
Jules Vernes
Julian Hawthrone
Julie A Lippmann
Justin Huntly McCarthy
Kakuzo Okakura
Karle Wilson Baker
Kate Chopin
Kenneth Grahame
Kenneth McGaffey
Kate Langley Bosher
Kate Langley Bosher
Katherine Cecil Thurston
Katherine Stokes
L. A. Abbot
L. T. Meade

L. Frank Baum
Latta Griswold
Laura Dent Crane
Laura Lee Hope
Laurence Housman
Lawrence Beasley
Leo Tolstoy
Leonid Andreyev
Lewis Carroll
Lewis Sperry Chafer
Lilian Bell
Lloyd Osbourne
Louis Hughes
Louis Joseph Vance
Louis Tracy
Louisa May Alcott
Lucy Fitch Perkins
Lucy Maud Montgomery
Luther Benson
Lydia Miller Middleton
Lyndon Orr
M. Corvus
M. H. Adams
Margaret E. Sangster
Margret Howth
Margaret Vandercook
Margaret W. Hungerford
Margret Penrose
Maria Edgeworth
Maria Thompson Daviess
Mariano Azuela
Marion Polk Angellotti
Mark Overton
Mark Twain
Mary Austin
Mary Catherine Crowley
Mary Cole
Mary Hastings Bradley
Mary Roberts Rinehart
Mary Rowlandson
M. Wollstonecraft Shelley
Maud Lindsay
Max Beerbohm
Myra Kelly
Nathaniel Hawthrone
Nicolo Machiavelli
O. F. Walton
Oscar Wilde

Owen Johnson
P.G. Wodehouse
Paul and Mabel Thorne
Paul G. Tomlinson
Paul Severing
Percy Brebner
Percy Keese Fitzhugh
Peter B. Kyne
Plato
Quincy Allen
R. Derby Holmes
R. L. Stevenson
R. S. Ball
Rabindranath Tagore
Rahul Alvares
Ralph Bonehill
Ralph Henry Barbour
Ralph Victor
Ralph Waldo Emmerson
Rene Descartes
Ray Cummings
Rex Beach
Rex E. Beach
Richard Harding Davis
Richard Jefferies
Richard Le Gallienne
Robert Barr
Robert Frost
Robert Gordon Anderson
Robert L. Drake
Robert Lansing
Robert Lynd
Robert Michael Ballantyne
Robert W. Chambers
Rosa Nouchette Carey
Rudyard Kipling
Saint Augustine
Samuel B. Allison
Samuel Hopkins Adams
Sarah Bernhardt
Sarah C. Hallowell
Selma Lagerlof
Sherwood Anderson
Sigmund Freud
Standish O'Grady
Stanley Weyman
Stella Benson
Stella M. Francis

Stephen Crane
Stewart Edward White
Stijn Streuvels
Swami Abhedananda
Swami Parmananda
T. S. Ackland
T. S. Arthur
The Princess Der Ling
Thomas A. Janvier
Thomas A Kempis
Thomas Anderton
Thomas Bailey Aldrich
Thomas Bulfinch
Thomas De Quincey
Thomas Dixon
Thomas H. Huxley
Thomas Hardy
Thomas More
Thornton W. Burgess
U. S. Grant
Upton Sinclair
Valentine Williams
Various Authors
Vaughan Kester
Victor Appleton
Victor G. Durham
Victoria Cross
Virginia Woolf
Wadsworth Camp
Walter Camp
Walter Scott
Washington Irving
Wilbur Lawton
Wilkie Collins
Willa Cather
Willard F. Baker
William Dean Howells
William le Queux
W. Makepeace Thackeray
William W. Walter
William Shakespeare
Winston Churchill
Yei Theodora Ozaki
Yogi Ramacharaka
Young E. Allison
Zane Grey

www.ingramcontent.com/pod-product-compliance
Lightning Source LLC
Chambersburg PA
CBHW051824170626
46807CB00003B/1022